GEN RYAN

MORE FROM GEN RYAN

THIN RED LINES SERIES
Beautiful Masterpiece (#1)
Beautiful Sacrifice (#2)
Beautiful Torment (#3)

TRADE ME COLLECTION (GAY ROMANCE)
Fix You
Losing You

HOPELESSLY DEVOTED SERIES
When We Were Young (#1)
Out of Goodbyes (#2)
More Than Words (#3)
She's Everything (#4)

STAND-ALONE NOVELS
Three Empty Words

This is part 2 of Parker's story, the continuation of *More Than Words*.
It is essential you read *More Than Words* first before reading this final part.

She's Everything © 2018 by Gen Ryan

All rights reserved. No part of this book may be used or reproduced in any written, electronic, recorded, or photocopied format without the express permission from the author or publisher as allowed under the terms and conditions with which it was purchased or as strictly permitted by applicable copyright law. Any unauthorized distribution, circulation or use of this text may be a direct infringement of the author's rights, and those responsible may be liable in law accordingly. Thank you for respecting the work of this author.

She's Everything is a work of fiction. All names, characters, events and places found therein are either from the author's imagination or used fictitiously. Any similarity to persons alive or dead, actual events, locations, or organizations is entirely coincidental and not intended by the author.

For information, contact the publisher, Hot Tree Publishing.

WWW.HOTTREEPUBLISHING.COM
EDITING: HOT TREE EDITING
COVER DESIGNER: SOXSATIONAL COVER ART
FORMATTER: RMGRAPHX

ISBN: 978-1-925655-78-0

*To love. May everyone go after it, cherish it,
and rejoice in it.
Love is always the answer.*

1 Corinthians 13:4-8

Love is patient, love is kind. It does not envy, it does not boast, it is not proud. It does not dishonor others, it is not self-seeking, it is not easily angered, it keeps no record of wrongs. Love does not delight in evil but rejoices with the truth. It always protects, always trusts, always hopes, always perseveres.

CHAPTER ONE

Arya

I always dreamt of being a mother. While my childhood was filled with happiness and good times, and my parents loved my brother, Justin, and me so much, it had sometimes been stifling. I thought of how I'd be different from them as a parent, though. I'd chase the happiness and good times. Never make choices for them or project my own thoughts or feelings on what they wanted to do with their life. I had it all figured out until I got pregnant and all those ideas seemed stupid.

My child wasn't even the size of a pea yet and I was already crazy in love and fiercely protective. I'd do anything for my baby's happiness. And the one thing in the craziness of my life I was absolutely sure about was that seeing the baby smile every day of their life was my new goal.

Rubbing my stomach, I knew that all those earlier thoughts were a load of shit. Making the decision to walk out on the man I loved wasn't something that came easily. The old Arya would have thrown herself into Parker's healing. Suffered through it all with him. But I'd been watching him these past weeks as he grieved for his sister, Emily. Even before her death being with him was a roller coaster of emotions. I didn't know this person growing inside of me, but I would do anything to protect my child, even from its father who would rather die than be a part of our life.

"Knock, knock." I heard my mother's voice before she came into focus. Lifting my head off my pillow, my vision still blurry from all the crying, I felt the bed dip. "How are you holding up, sweetie?" My mother brushed back my hair.

"Eh." I shrugged for fear that if I said anything else, I'd completely lose it. I wanted my happily ever after. The picture-perfect family I'd seen in my mind when I was a young girl. Yet here I was, pregnant, with a partner who was struggling so badly that I knew I couldn't help him. Parker hated himself and his past so much that he didn't want to go on. I wanted to be enough for him. To be the one to make him see the world as beautiful and worth living. But I wasn't.

Why aren't I enough?

"Well, you can stay here as long as you need." She patted my hand.

"I'm pregnant, Mom," I whispered. I hadn't told anyone but Emily and my sister-in-law, Mona, about my pregnancy. I wanted to surprise my parents with this epic reveal, but that idea had gone to shit. I'd been petrified of Parker's reaction, and all my fears were solidified tonight when he let me go. He let *us* go.

"Oh my God." My mother jumped up and squealed with excitement. She paced frantically, making plans, but stopped and looked down at me. "Is that why you and Parker fought? Over the baby?" Her eyes widened, and I saw tears glistening in her eyes. I knew she was thinking the worst of Parker and while I wanted to defend him, I wasn't sure I could. He made it clear he thought he'd be a shit father before he even knew, and when I told him I was pregnant, there was no emotion in his eyes. Just emptiness. The same as it had been for weeks.

"Yes and no. He had pills lined up like he was going to take them all. I lost it. The thought of bringing a baby into that life, with a father who doesn't want to be alive, it tore me up. I just wanted everything to be perfect. I pictured telling Parker and him finally getting out of bed and not mourning the loss of Emily. But it didn't happen that way. He let me go." Tears welled in my eyes before they streamed down, wracking through my body. My shoulders shook with my sadness, anger, and frustrations. "He let us both walk out that door." I barely got the words out between my sobs. I gripped at my stomach. This poor child wouldn't deserve this life. Every child deserved love and affection from both parents, not wondering why one didn't love them enough to be part of their life.

What was left of my heart was breaking. How was I going to be the mother I always wanted to be when I was hurting so badly?

"Arya." My mother took me in her arms. "You have good instincts and I have no doubt that you made the right choice in leaving. Parker is a complex, thoughtful man with a troubled past. Much deeper I think than even you know. He'll come around."

I looked up at my mother. "What if he doesn't?" That was my fear. That I was going to do this alone. To have to look in my child's eyes and pretend that I was enough for them as a mother when I wasn't enough for Parker. I don't know why I thought he would change for me. I knew firsthand what depression and addiction did to a person, but the thought was there. I won't deny it. I wanted to be enough.

But I wasn't.

"Then you raise this baby as the strong, independent woman I know you are. Parker doesn't define your happiness. He just happened to be a man who made you happy."

My mother was being rational, but I didn't want that right now. I wanted my sadness and pain. Most of all, I wanted Parker. The way he made me feel when things were good. The baking sessions and making love on every surface in the house while we constantly told one another we loved each other. When he smiled, laughed and wanted to live. When life was worth living.

"Why does it have to be like this? We were so happy."

I sniffed and rested my head on my mother's shoulder.

"Because mental illness isn't kind. You know this firsthand. Parker has seen things that no person should ever have to see. And then losing his sister right when things were going so well?" My mother shook her head, a few tears falling that she brushed away. "He's hurting. He feels things deeper than the average person. Which is both good and bad. The way he looks at you, there is no doubt in my mind he loves you. But with the good emotions comes the bad. And those can be hard to process."

Her words hit me hard. Parker did feel things on a deeper level. His writing spoke about the pain he hid from the world, and even the happiness.

"I shouldn't have left him. He needs me." I sat up and rubbed my eyes. How was Parker going to get better with me here?

"No. You're staying right here." My mother and I looked up and saw my father in the doorway with his arms across his chest.

"But—"

He held up his hand to stop me. "Parker is a good guy, but he needs to get his shit together before he deserves you and the precious gift of a child. Let him work for it. Alone."

I glanced at my mother who nodded.

"Parker had Rainey, from what you explained, to always help him. Now you. He's never been able to be independent or take control of his own life. He needs to realize he can do it on this own." My father came into my room and gave me a hug. I tensed at first when my father hugged me, but then I softened. My parents were everything to me. Even in my struggles they never gave up on me. Faith. Love. Tough love got me through. But in the end, I had them to help me. I left, and now Parker had no one. I couldn't help but question whether I'd done the right thing. "It's all going to work out just fine," my father added. I hoped he was right.

"How do you know, Dad?" I listened to his heartbeat, steady, constant. My father had always been that for me. Even when he was answering the phone and fielding boys when I was younger. He did it all out of love. I never doubted that.

"Because Justin is on his way over there now."

"What?" I jumped up. "He's going to kill him."

"Motivation." He smiled and rubbed my stomach. "I'm going to be a grandpa again." His eyes filled with tears.

I looked at my parents, absorbed the love and support they offered. If things between Parker and me didn't work out, I knew soul deep that our child would have a good life, filled with people who loved them more than anything in the world. It may not be the vision I had in my mind when I was young and naïve, but it'd be exactly what it needed to be. Because it was love that mattered most. Feeling comforted and cared for. And no matter what, we'd have that, because my family would never give anything less.

CHAPTER TWO

Parker

I had no expectations for my life when I was a child. It was all about survival. Emily and I fought daily to find food to eat and clothes to wear. We fought against the physical abuse that often came when our parents drank too much. So, living a life of happiness? Being in love? That shit was never on my mind. And once I got a taste of happiness with Rainey and then Arya, it came as no surprise that I fucked it up.

Numb, my mind whirled with thoughts of becoming a father, something I never knew beyond beatings and harsh words. How was I going to be a father, loving, kind, and supportive when I couldn't even see beyond my own pain? It was crippling, and I was succumbing to the pressure of just trying to survive. Surviving was something I had done my entire life but I no longer knew how. It was Emily who kept me going when I was younger. She needed food, I got us food any way

I could. I'd steal. Borrow. Beg. I worked before I legally could. She gave me purpose. Now I felt like all my drive, my motivation, was taken from me when Emily died. I knew I needed to find that again. For my child. For Arya. The woman who came into my life unexpectedly and made me believe in second chances. I needed to find my strength so I could be everything she thought I could be. A man not defined by his PTSD and past that haunted him.

A better man.

Gripping the side of the wall, I lifted myself off the floor and stared at my reflection in the mirror. Everything was different. My hair was longer. My face that used to always be clean-shaven had week-old stubble. My time off from work ended tomorrow and I had to get myself together. I couldn't live with myself if I lost my job too. I could barely live with myself now.

"You look like absolute shit." I jumped. Justin stood in the doorway to the bathroom, shaking his head.

"Thanks." I rubbed the scruff on my face. "How the hell did you get in here?"

Justin held keys out in front of him and jingled them. "Arya gave me her set. Or rather, I took them from her purse." He shrugged like rifling through his sister's purse was nothing.

"What do you want, Justin? To tell me that I'm a fuckup? To finally punch me in the face like you wanted to when we first met? It's a little late. I know I fucked up. Know that I just let the two most important things that ever came into my life walk out that door." I gripped the sides of the sink to keep myself upright. I felt drunk, yet I'd had nothing to drink. Whiskey screamed my name to drown the sorrow that coursed through me like poison. I wanted relief, but fuck me if I knew how to get it.

"No." Justin sighed and shoved the keys in his pocket. "I didn't come to beat you up. I didn't come to tell you any of that. You're beating yourself up enough on your own." He paused. "Come on. Let's go sit and have a chat. It's been a long time coming." He motioned to me with his chin. Reluctantly, I let go of the sink and followed behind him. We sat at my kitchen table, across from each other.

Silence clung to us for a while, and I watched Justin struggle. He rubbed his face a few times before finally saying what seemed to be bothering him so much.

"Fuck. This sucks, man," Justin said as he leaned forward and shoved his face in his hands. "I tried so hard to forget what happened to Arya… at the hands of my best friend. But it's like a damn sickness that keeps coming back."

I held up my hands and shook my head. "Justin, we don't have to talk about this. I know what happened."

"No. You know how it happened to Arya. But not me. Her brother. The person who should have protected her. I fell asleep. Oblivious to the true asshole that my best friend was. I knew he was a womanizer. Liked sex.

But I never thought he'd cross that line. He did. And to this day I regret falling asleep that night." Justin voice broke and he cleared his throat. "As brothers we have this ingrained sense of having to be the ultimate protector for our sisters. I know you felt that with Emily." I nodded and hung my head. Everything Justin was saying was true. I was fiercely protective of Emily, and when she died, I took that to heart. Like I was the one who killed her because I wasn't there. I failed as a big brother. "Life has its own agenda. No matter what we do, how we change things, or how hard we try to protect them, something can happen in a flash. It isn't your fault, what happened to Emily. You would have done anything for her. Anyone could see that. But now, you're going to be a father. That child needs you. And as much as it scared me at first when Arya said she was in love with you, someone with such a troubled past, she needs you too. You need each other."

I leaned back in my chair and took in Justin's words. They were honest and heartfelt, and it made me understand him in a much better light. He may have given me a hard time when we first met, but it was for Arya, to protect her from exactly what I was putting her through now. Justin surprised me though, by coming here and talking to me. I figured a swift punch in the throat would have sufficed, but he wanted Arya to be happy. I did have a troubled past, and with Arya's own issues, we could have been disastrous together, but we weren't. We were imperfect but blissful. Broken but mendable. We were soul mates, and Justin helped me realize all that she was worth.

"You're not responsible for what happened to Arya either. I think we both took a lot of the blame for situations that weren't our fault," I added. I moved closer to Justin, not sure whether to hug him or give him a punch on the shoulder. I wasn't good with expressing myself verbally. Words on paper were more my thing.

"You're right. I'm not responsible. But I will spend the rest of my life being the big brother I wish I always was to her." Justin squared his shoulders.

I had spent the last year with Emily mending our broken past. Trying so hard to make amends for leaving her and trying to pretend her addictions and my mental illness didn't exist.

God, I hope she knew how much I loved her.

"I don't know if I can," I whispered, my tears freely falling. Normally I would be self-conscious about crying around someone, but with what Justin and I were sharing, I didn't care how he saw me. This was how I felt. Conflicted. Emotional. Afraid. I was vulnerable and it scared the shit out of me.

"You can. Emily is a part of you. She'll be a part of your baby. Prove to her that you can be the man she always knew you could be."

I wanted to be a better man. To tackle my PTSD, not mask the symptoms with baking and pretend smiling. The thing was, I didn't know how.

"I don't know how." I was ashamed of my words, but they were the truth. All I knew was cuss words, alcohol, and war.

"That's okay. I'm going to help you." Justin smiled.

I shook my head. "Why?" I scoffed in disbelief.

"For Arya. Because like I said, she loves you. Why, I'll never know," he mumbled.

I rolled my eyes and he offered me a smile. This was the Justin I was accustomed to, the smartass who liked to fuck around with me. I was happy that we had this conversation but thankful that some of the heaviness was replaced with his normal snarkiness.

"How is she?" I played with the end of the table. I hated how she'd seen me and how we left things. She was doing what she had to in order to protect our child, and all I'd thought of was myself. If she hadn't walked in on me though, who knew what could have happened, if I'd even be sitting here to have this conversation with Justin.

"Heartbroken," he said matter-of-factly.

"I have to go to her. Apologize." I stood up, the chair scuffing against the floor.

"No. Not yet. Give it time. Work on getting better." Justin pointed to the chair and I sat back down with a huff.

"She needs to know I love her. And the baby. I don't want her to think I deserted them."

"Fair enough. You can grovel. But prove it, man. The best gift you can give your family is fixing what's screwing with your mind. You can't be the father, partner, or police officer you want to be until you are able to do what you need to."

It all seemed so simple. Do what I needed to, but just like when Arya tried to peel back my layers, I wanted to run and hide. I wouldn't though, because I wanted to be a father. Not like mine who taught me nothing but how badly I wanted to get out of my shitty life. I wanted my child to look up at me with pride and love, and know that even though I may not be perfect, I tried so damn hard to be the best father I could be. The one thing I did have was love. So much fucking love to give that it strangled me. Despite what some people said, love was enough. And I was about to fucking prove it. Arya and I were going to live happily ever after. Someday. I was going to work my ass off to get us there, and it would be worth it, because she changed the rules on me. Made me want to open up and be more than words on paper and emotions that seeped through the ink. She made me want a family. She made me want to be a better man, and gave me hope that maybe I could be a better father than my own.

CHAPTER THREE

Arya

I was waiting by the front door as soon as my parents told me that Justin was coming over to drop off Nicholas so he and Mona could go see a movie. He'd been dodging my questions about how Parker was doing and what he'd said to him. It was driving me crazy. My mind had gone to some pretty dark places thinking of all that Parker was probably going through. And I wasn't there. I made that choice, and since I walked out that door, I'd regretted leaving. What did that say about me, that I left him when things were so bad? Did that make me a horrible person? Depression I could live with. Even help him through. But when I walked in on those pills lined up, the thought of him taking his life scared me. It wasn't just about me anymore, because I would have stayed. It was about our child and ensuring that they got the life they deserved.

I moved to the front window and peeled back the

curtain to get a better look. The curse of being short was that I could barely see out the front door window.

"Arya, get away from the window. The neighbors will think you're crazy." My mother laughed. Draping her arm around my shoulder, she gave me a squeeze. "Don't you want to help me bake some brownies?" My weakness, baking. Just when I was about to agree, I saw Justin's car pull into the driveway.

"I will. As soon as I get information out of Justin." I swung open the front door and glared at him as he walked toward me.

"If looks could kill…." Justin winked while Nicholas cooed in his arms.

"You're lucky you're holding my nephew." I snickered.

"Not for long." My mother bypassed us and stole Nicholas away. "Come on, baby. Let's go make some brownies and let your aunty yell at your daddy." We watched as they walked down the hall to the kitchen and were out of earshot.

"Arya, listen, I didn't kill him. He's safe. Just like I said a thousand times via text message." Justin held up his hands and took a step back.

"How did he look though? Did he get out of bed?" I may have walked out on Parker but my feelings for him were stronger than ever. I wanted him to get better and to see that there was life outside of the depression he had been living in for the greater part of his life.

Justin's arms flew up in frustration. "Jesus Christ.

He looked like a man who lost his sister. Who's struggling, but going to do what it takes to get better. Let the man do what he needs to do to prove that he's everything you deserve." Justin rubbed his face and sighed.

The anger I expected wasn't there. I swallowed back the bubble of emotion, because he was right. I was being obsessive, but the last thing I wanted Parker to do was harm himself.

Damn. I hated when my brother was right.

"Okay. I just don't want him to hurt himself. I love him. So much." I wrapped my arms around myself. I pretended they were Parker's arms, firm and strong around me like they had been not that long before. He had so much strength, sometimes more than I think he even knew. He just had to find it.

Bringing me in for a hug, Justin held me tight. "I know. And he loves you too. You have to give him time." I melted into my brother's arms. He rubbed my back and let me stay there for a few moments. Usually he'd be scurrying away and pretending that we didn't just have a heart-to-heart, but I needed this, and the way he held me told me that he knew that.

I nodded. "I will."

"Good. Now go help Mom bake brownies. Mona and I need to catch the movie. I love you and want what's best for you. Parker can be that. Have faith."

Leaning in, Justin kissed my cheek. We weren't generally overly affectionate, so Justin's words meant a lot to me.

"What do you know about faith, Justin Danvers?" I giggled, trying to make light of the situation.

He looked right at me, his eyes pinned to mine. He gaze was intense, and I immediately stopped laughing.

"After the shit that happened to you, I feared you'd never come back to us. That you'd never be the carefree, happy, loving-life girl you were before that scumbag raped you." Where normally I would have cringed at these words, I didn't. I stood tall and listened to my brother tell me how the night that irrevocably changed my life impacted his. It's hard when faced with a trauma like I had been to realize that it impacts other people. I was so deep in my own grief that I failed to realize those around me suffered too.

"But you did. It was trying and difficult to watch you struggle, but we had faith. And here you are. Beautiful. In love, and about to be a mother."

Tears streamed down my face and I reached out for Justin again. This time, I brought him against me. He tensed at first, but then loosened up a bit.

"Thank you for being there for me. Always."

Justin and I separated and he nodded, shuffling from foot to foot. I knew our conversation was close to an end.

"You may have some OCD when it comes to baking, but I'm not mad about it." He patted his stomach.

As we both laughed, Mona's voice sounded from outside.

"Babe, we're going to miss the movie!" she called out.

"I got to go for real. Just know that Parker is trying. Just like you did."

With a nod, I watched Justin and Mona drive away and relished his words. I'd have faith because just like he said, I was able to shift through my own demons and make it to the other side. I'd have faith in Parker because despite what he thought, I knew he was strong and fierce. He'd pull through. If not for me, then for our child who would be the greatest thing to happen to either of us. I knew it.

***

"Isn't this the cutest?" Mona held out a pair of infant shoes for me to see.

"They're adorable." She threw them in the cart. "Mona, we have no idea what I'm having." I laughed.

"It's a girl. I know these things." She flitted her hand like anything else was an absurd thought. She leaned down and spoke to Nicholas, who was sitting in his stroller.

"I hope it's a girl," my mother said as she looked at the clothes. "Look at this pink tutu!" She threw it in the cart on top of the shoes. "Oh! We should look at cribs and stuff too. I'll buy you the crib."

"Guys!" I sighed. "Chill, please." My mother and Mona paused and looked at me. "I'd like to have something to do with Parker. When he comes around." I bit my lip before turning and shuffling through the clothes on the rack for a distraction.

"Of course, dear." My mother gave me a side hug.

The thought of Parker missing out on anything made my heart ache. It'd only been a few days since I left, and I so badly wanted to see his face, hear his voice. Justin was right, though. Parker needed time, and while I so badly wanted to fix him, I couldn't. He had to do that on his own.

"But maybe we peek at maternity clothes? I'll need them before you know it." I had to live, even though it killed me to think of doing parts of this without Parker. My family was here, present, and so excited for my journey into parenthood. They deserved to be excited. So, looking at maternity clothes I could do. The rest would have to wait.

"Yay!" Mona said. Nicholas clapped from his stroller and we all laughed. With Mona leading the way, we all walked toward maternity clothes.

"You're going to be a great mom," Mom said as she readjusted her purse.

"You think so?" I looked over at her as we continued walking.

"I know so. You always played house as a child. It's something that always came naturally to you. That and baking," she teased.

Motherhood was something I always wanted. Baking was something I always loved. I was about to have both. Excitement fluttered deep in my stomach, anticipation mixed with apprehension. But the fact was, I knew how to love and my child would never feel anything but.

"Look at this dress! You'd look adorable in this." Mona and my mother fussed over me, and I let them. I wanted their excitement. Their joy. Because despite my concern for Parker, my pregnancy was a blessing. And this blessing was worth everything, even leaving the man I loved to ensure the life of our child was wonderful and pure.

CHAPTER FOUR

Parker

Time to start getting my shit together. The first step in getting said shit together was not looking like a caveman. There was a long list of shit I had to do, counseling being right at the top, but I had to start with not looking like I often felt, like a failure.

"This is going to hurt like a bitch." Placing a more than generous amount of shaving cream on my face, I held the razor in my hand and braced myself. Taking the razor down my skin, I fought back a scream.

It was like the pain of a thousand suns raking across my face.

Goddammit, why did I let this grow out?

"Jesus," I said as I watched the hair hit the sink. All in the name of love, right? I'd do anything for Arya. Shit, I'd shave myself dry if it meant that she'd take my sorry ass back after all I put her through. It was taking every ounce of me to not crawl over to her parents' house now and stand outside of her window with a boom box and profess my love.

After I finished shaving, I had a few hours until I had to be at work. It'd be my first shift back since Emily died. Part of me was ready to go back, another part craved the silence and the solace of this apartment. In the interest of moving forward, I had to get back into the swing of things.

I hovered outside Emily's bedroom door, the one place I still couldn't bring myself to go in since she had passed. Holding the doorknob in my hand, I took a deep breath—and entered. The air was stagnant and still, but it smelled like her. She always wore some perfume that would clear out your nostrils and singe your nose hairs. It was her signature scent and one of the many things I loved about her. So much about Emily was routine and structured. She kept her room clean, even though other parts of her life were chaotic. She wore the same perfume, same pale pink lipstick, and same black boots every day. All those things sat on her bedroom floor. A painful reminder that she was gone.

I stood in the center of her room, not knowing where to start or what to do. The room couldn't stay like this forever. It was a shrine to my sister. But I didn't need it anymore. She was in my memories. In my heart. She was everything that was good about my childhood, and I'd carry her with me every day, wherever I went.

"I miss you," I said as I started pulling out boxes from under her bed and shifting through things. Emily may have seemed organized, but she was a hoarder. The few pictures from our childhood, she had tucked away in boxes. I put those pictures aside and kept going through my sister's life. She'd been so young. Had so much of life left to live. I'd lost so many people in my life you'd think I'd be a pro at it, but it never got easier. Each loss sent me closer and closer to the edge. Just when I'd thought I was free from the heartache, Emily died and I spiraled. If it wasn't for Arya and the fact that when I closed my eyes I saw her smiling face, I would have gone over that edge. Just like I had said from the beginning, Arya saved my life and didn't even know it. She was slowly pulling me away from the edge that I wanted to jump from. I never wanted to go back there.

I thought that nothing made sense after Emily's death, but her death brought a clarity I never knew I could have. I wanted to live. To love. And I'd do anything to feel whole and worthy of those things.

The familiar itch in my hands came. Words touched my lips and begged to be heard. As if Emily knew, a piece of paper and pen sat on the side of her bed. I didn't touch them. Not tonight, because like Arya said, I needed to be more than words. I had to show her that she was everything to me.

***

Walking into the police station, I tried my best to hold my head up high and fight against the panic that I felt rising in my chest. I wanted to be better, but that didn't happen overnight. So I would fight every day to change, and that started with getting back to my routine and fighting against my demons.

"Well, look what the cat dragged in." Ross finished making his coffee and headed toward me. He slapped my shoulder and gave me a smile. "You doing okay?"

Ross and almost the entire department were there at Emily's funeral. He had been a pall bearer and there for me through it all. That brought Ross and me closer, even though we weren't as close as I'd been with Jon and Cooper. I was thankful for him being my partner and being there for me. It had been a while since I had a friend.

"I'm getting there. Finally got out of bed."

Ross laughed and handed me his coffee. "Take it. Looks like you need it." He frowned.

"Yeah. Not sleeping too well. Arya left." I took a sip of the coffee that tasted more like swill than caffeine.

"*Left* left?" We moved toward the coffee station for a bit more privacy. The hustle of the police department was welcome, as it drowned out our voices and a conversation I'd rather not have others overhear.

"Yeah. I was in a bad spot. Did some stupid shit. Now I'm trying to figure out how to win her back."

Ross shook his head. "Damn, Parker. I'm sorry.

Nothing like being hit when you're down."

I didn't want people to villainize Arya. For some it might seem like she left me when I needed her the most, but that wasn't it at all. I gave her no choice.

"No, she had every right to leave. I was miserable. Depressed. A certifiable asshole." I hung my head in shame. "And she's pregnant."

Ross's eyes shot up to mine. "Wow. Congratulations. Daddy Parker."

"Daddy." I said the word; it seemed foreign on my lips.

"You okay with that?" Ross sipped his coffee, picking up on my hesitation.

"I don't know. I want to be. Didn't have the best role model growing up. Still finding it hard to get out of bed somedays. It's difficult to think of getting this precious gift that I can so easily screw up."

Ross frowned. "Don't do that, man. If anyone deserves a bit of light in their life, it's you. Being a father is the greatest thing. If that doesn't make you want to kick your ass into gear, nothing will."

My phone vibrated, and I checked the text from Justin telling me that Arya had a doctor's appointment tomorrow for the baby. He didn't leave any expectations. He simply put the ball in my court.

"You're right, Ross. How'd you get so smart?" I teased.

"I became a father at seventeen years old. That little girl put me on the straight and narrow."

"No shit?" I didn't know he was a father. He never spoke about his daughter, even after all the time we'd spent together.

"She lives with her mother and stepfather. But the time we get together, it makes all the shit I went through in my life worth it." The way he spoke about his daughter, I couldn't help but smile. His voice was softer, his face kinder. Ross was right, being a father did change you.

Our radios went off for a domestic disturbance, interrupting our conversation.

"Well, time to rock and roll," Ross said, changing the subject effortlessly.

Ross had helped me more than he realized. I knew that being father, while scary, was going to be the greatest gift. Getting Arya back wouldn't be easy, but I'd start with showing her how much I was ready for this next chapter in my life and how badly I wanted us to take this journey together. To be the family she dreamed of. To be the family I never knew I wanted.

CHAPTER FIVE

Arya

I wasn't sure if excited was the right word to use, but the moment was bittersweet. Today was the baby's first doctor's appointment and I was alone. I stared at all the other couples, laughing, smiling, and looking at baby magazines. After what happened with Parker, and me making the decision to leave, we hadn't spoken in a few days. I kept checking my phone hoping for a call or an "I'm sorry" text message. They never came. I wasn't sure what I'd expected, but part of me wished I'd wake up and all of this would be a bad dream.

"Arya Danvers?" Gathering my purse, I walked toward the nurse who held my chart close to her chest. "I'm Angela and will be your nurse. Just you today?" she asked as she looked past me. My eyes welled up with tears and the lump in my throat threatened to strangle me.

I was alone. My hand went to my stomach.

Just you and me, baby.

"No. She's not alone." Parker hustled to catch up with us and smiled at me. It wasn't a full smile that reached across his face; it stopped, showing his hesitation. My throat went dry and my stomach fluttered. He was here. While my doubts were still there, the fact that Parker showed up spoke volumes. He cared. He was trying. And damn, did he look good doing it.

"And you are?" Angela asked.

"Parker Matthews. The father," Parker said proudly. I'd seen the same look in his eyes when he graduated the police academy, happiness mixed with awe and appreciation. This time though, it was not an appreciation for all that he accomplished to become an officer, it was for this life that was not yet plagued by all the troubles Parker and I had experienced. Awe for a life that we created together. Our eyes met and there was none of the hesitation that was there when he first announced his presence. He was confident and proud. I was at a loss for words. I had no idea how Parker knew about the appointment. I stared at him intently. His face was clean-shaven and he wore a pair of jeans and a nice button-up shirt. He looked good. Healthy. A far cry from the last time I saw him. He looked like the man I fell in love with.

"Is this a problem, Arya?" Angela asked as we walked into a room.

I wasn't expecting him to be here, but it brought me comfort to not be alone. My mother wanted to come, but I told her that I needed to do this by myself. Really, I wanted Parker. My partner. The man I loved.

"No. It's not a problem at all." I sat on the exam table and Parker took a seat right next to me.

"Great. I'm going to ask some questions."

After answering what was the equivalent to my life history, Angela left us alone while we waited for Dr. Sanderson.

"What are you doing here, Parker?" I folded my hands in my lap to resist the urge to reach out and touch him. I noticed that his hair had been trimmed. He was taking steps in the right direction.

"Justin told me about the appointment. He figured I wouldn't want to miss it." Parker gave a half smile. His leg shook, jarring the chair he was sitting in.

"Are you okay?" I motioned to his leg.

"Oh. Yeah. Sorry." His leg stopped shaking. "Just nervous."

"About?"

"This?" He shrugged. "I'm not sure what to expect. I just want the baby to be healthy." I closed my eyes. "I want you to be healthy and happy, too." Opening my eyes, I saw Parker had moved to stand in front of me, his arms on either side of the exam table. There was no way out. Not that I wanted to escape. But Parker could be so intense and right now, his eyes were dark and hungry as he looked down at me. I licked my lips, causing him to groan.

"You said you didn't want kids, Parker," I reminded him. He couldn't just waltz in here and pretend that he hadn't hurt me. That the thought of being a father didn't scare him.

"I said a lot of things I regret. But my biggest regret is letting you walk out that door." I sucked in a sharp breath. "I'm sorry for that. For letting the death of Emily spoil what should have been happy news in our life. Because this is our life. Together. Me. You. This baby." Gently he placed his hand on my stomach.

I shook my head. I wanted to believe him, but I couldn't live with the thought that what I witnessed could happen again. "I don't know…." I bit the side of my mouth.

"It's okay, baby." He tucked my hair behind my ear. "I'm going to prove to you that I deserve to be in your life. And our child's life. For now, know that I love you both more than anything in the world. You're the reason I got out of bed the past few days. Your smile. Your laugh. And the thought of holding our child in my arms gives me hope. You both are everything to me. Fucking everything."

He brushed a tear away before a knock sounded at the door.

"Hello!" Dr. Sanderson came in, cheery and excited. "I can't believe you're going to have a baby!" she said. Dr. Sanderson had been my OBGYN since I was sixteen years old. I was glad to have her with me on this journey.

"I know." I smiled as Parker retook his seat next to me. My mind still reeled with his words. He was always so good with words. I wanted more.

"Who's this hunk of man?" Dr. Sanderson shook Parker's hand.

"My…." I hesitated.

"Boyfriend," Parker finished.

"Wonderful." She clapped her hands. "All right. Let's take a listen and hear this baby's heartbeat, shall we? Lie back, please."

She lifted up my shirt and placed some gel that was colder than ice on my stomach. I sucked in my breath, my belly going hollow.

"Sorry, it's always so cold." She laughed as she placed the heart monitor on my stomach.

Then we heard it, the gentle thump of our baby's heartbeat.

"There it is," Dr. Sanderson said. "Strong little one."

Parker stood up and got closer, his hand finding its way to mine. He squeezed, and I looked up, seeing the tears glistening in his eyes.

"That's our baby's heartbeat?" he asked.

"It sure is. Everything sounds wonderful." Dr. Sanderson took a cloth and wiped off the gel.

"That's it? I want to keep listening," Parker complained.

My heart swelled. This man, he may not have been without flaws, but his love was pure and heartfelt. It was everything I knew it would be the moment I saw him in that classroom and fell in love with his words. And right then I wanted nothing but to be in his arms.

"Next appointment you'll get to see the baby on ultrasound," Dr. Sanderson said through a laugh. "Are you guys interested in parenting classes? Lamaze, any of that?" She took out her script book.

Parker helped me sit up and before I could reply, he did.

"We want it all. We're doing this right," he said proudly, with another squeeze of my hand.

"All right. I'll have Angela get you the information. Here's a prescription for prenatal vitamins. Be sure to take them daily." Dr. Sanderson handed me a prescription.

"Thank you." I smiled as she walked out of the room. "That was incredible." I stared at Parker in awe. There was a human being growing inside of me. That we made together. No matter what happened between us, I knew that was a gift, something to be cherished and loved.

"I never knew a sound that sweet existed." Parker rubbed my hand. My body tingled with desire. Arousal was too tame a word to describe the sensations shooting through me. Between my legs throbbed, my nipples hardened, and I'd have given anything to have Parker right there and then.

"I want you," I said. He backed away and my brow dipped. "What?" My heart thumped against my chest.

"I want you too. So bad." He brought my hand down to his hard dick and I blushed. "But I don't deserve you. Not yet. But I will. I promise I'll work so damn hard to prove to you that I can be the man you need and the man you deserve. Both of you." Leaning down, he kissed my stomach.

How did I argue with that logic? Parker needed to do this. To get better and try to fight for what he wanted, and I wouldn't stand in his way. Even if I wanted his face between my legs and to feel his hands all over my body. We'd have a lifetime for that, a future together that I knew was going to be amazing. Because even though he was suffering, his resolve, the fact that he was standing here next to me, whispering promises to our unborn child, showed me that Parker Matthews was already changing, and it brought tears to my eyes and filled my heart with hope.

"Okay. I'll wait for you. I love you, Parker."

Kissing my stomach one last time, he gripped my cheeks in his hands. "I love you too. So much. I won't let you down again." The pain on Parker's face broke me.

I sprinkled kisses all over his face and pressed my forehead to his.

"The only person you have to worry about letting down is yourself. Be brave. Be strong and come back to us."

Our chests heaved as we stared at each other, only inches apart. The need to be physically closer was apparent, but we couldn't. Not yet. I respected Parker's desire to fight for us. To prove his worth. Little did he know, he had me back the moment he showed up to this appointment and had tears in his eyes at the sound of our child's heartbeat. Parker Matthews was everything, and I'd wait as long as it took for our happy ending.

CHAPTER SIX

Parker

There was nothing like hearing your child's heartbeat. In that moment, listening to the little thumps and looking down at the woman I loved, my life seemed to make sense. There wasn't an easy fix for all the shit I'd done in my life, shit that I'd rather forget and move on from, but that wouldn't be enough. Not this time. I wanted to do it right. Prove to not only Arya but to myself that I could move beyond the loss of Jon and Cooper and my own PTSD and find peace. Because listening to my baby's heartbeat, that was peace, tranquility, and love, and so much fucking more. It was everything I had been waiting for.

While I was still absolutely petrified of being a father, I'd try every day to be the best damn father because I had to. I wanted to. I needed to.

"So, the appointment went well?" Ross asked in between bites of cheeseburger.

"Yeah, man. It was good. Arya was surprised to see me."

"I'm glad you went. Even if things don't work out between you two, you need to be there for your kid." My back went rigid at his words. There was no way it wouldn't work out between Arya and me. That thought had never crossed my mind, and I was feeling a bit assholish that Ross even considered it.

"Things are going to work out just fine," I said between clenched teeth.

Ross nodded and held up his hands in defense. "Just trying to think of all possibilities."

"I appreciate the rational thoughts, but Arya and I made it clear to each other yesterday that we love each other and will be together." I threw the rest of my burger in the bag, losing my appetite. "I want to be the best version of myself when that happens. Because it will happen." I gripped the side of the car.

"Right." Ross took another big bite of his burger and looked out the window. No matter how many times I tried to find out what happened between him and his ex, he wouldn't delve into it, but he seemed bitter. Even hesitant to date. At least, I assumed that because he had dated no one since we'd met.

My phone dinged with an incoming message before I could say anything else on the subject.

Arya: I'm starving and this salad isn't cutting it. What I wouldn't give for a burger.

The message was accompanied by a selfie of her in

the break room at the high school with a sad face and a piece of lettuce hanging out of her mouth. I didn't reply; instead, I had the best idea.

"What would you say if we took Arya a burger and fries at work?"

Ross shrugged. "Ain't nothing better to do." He tapped his fingers against the steering wheel.

We went back through the drive-through and I got her burger meal, and then I stopped at the flower shop on the way to the high school. If I was going to surprise the girl I loved, I was going to do it in epic proportions.

"You can't just do anything small, can you?" Ross chuckled at the three dozen roses I stuffed in the back seat of the cruiser.

"Not when it comes to Arya and my kid. They deserve it all." I smiled at him. And I intended to give it to them for the rest of my life.

***

Okay. Maybe I didn't think this through. I was being ogled by a bunch of women, and I was sure even a few men as I checked myself in at the front desk.

"You're the guy Arya's been dating, aren't you?" I'd swear the older receptionist at the front batted her eyelashes at me.

"Yes, ma'am, I am." I tried to hold back my laughter

as two more women tried not to be nosey from their desks. One kept standing up and stretching; the other had gotten up to go to the trash can twice.

"Well, I'm Peggy. If you ever need anything or if you happen to have a younger officer friend who's single, I'm widowed and ready to get back out there." She blushed and gave me a wink.

"I'll let my very single partner know." I smiled.

"All right, Peggy." A younger woman came from the bigger office and held out her hand. "I'm Miss Ridgewood, the principal here." We shook hands. "We don't usually allow visitors for the staff, but Miss Danvers is in study hall and I suppose we can allow the exception." She gave me a terse smile.

I followed behind her, listening to her clanking heels against the tiled floor. I looked back at Peggy and shrugged at Miss Ridgewood's lack of conversation. She gave me a wave before I turned my attention back to Miss Stick in the Mud.

"Have you worked here long?" I asked, trying to make conversation.

"No" was all she said before she pointed to a closed door. "She's in there. I ask that you make it quick and don't disturb the students. Pleasure to meet you." She turned on her heels and walked away.

Damn. She couldn't have been much older than Arya and me, but acted like she legit had something stuck up her ass. Not letting her ruin my good mood, I peered through the small window in the door and saw

Arya in a pale yellow dress that instantly made me want to rip it off her. She looked gorgeous with her hair flowing around her, but the smile she wore was the best part.

A student pointed to the door and Arya looked up, our eyes connecting. That smile got wider and my heart soared. She loved me. I may not have deserved it, not yet, but her love for me was what kept me going. Kept me motivated. Made me want to change.

Arya stood up and opened the door. "I'll be right back. No funny business." She wiggled her finger at the class.

"Parker, what are you doing here?" Wrapping her arms around me, she kissed my cheek. I wanted her lips on mine, to press her up against the door and skim the bare skin that I knew was underneath her dress. It seemed like forever since I'd felt her skin against mine. Her softness. The way she responded to me instantly.

"I brought you"—I handed her the flowers—"and the baby"—then handed her the burger and fries—"some presents."

She smiled and sniffed the roses. "Here, hold this." She shoved the flowers back at me before tearing open the burger and taking a huge bite. "Oh my God, this is heaven." She moaned.

I laughed and kissed her forehead. "I'm glad you love it."

"It was a nice surprise."

I hugged her and fought back my laugh. In the

window to her classroom were a few faces of students, giggling and staring at us.

"What?" she asked as she turned around. She whipped the door open, and they all scurried back to their seats.

"Now, didn't I say to behave yourselves?" Arya's voice turned stern and I must admit, it was a turn-on.

"Yeah, Miss Danvers, but he's cute." A few teenage girls giggled.

"Well now, Officer Matthews, what do you have to say about that?" Arya chuckled.

"Thanks, I think?" I had followed her into the classroom and all eyes were on me.

"Officer Matthews writes poetry." Arya winked at me as the girls started whispering.

A boy in the front snickered.

"Care to share what's so funny, Billy?" Arya asked.

"Real men don't write poetry." He snickered again.

"Care to share something?" Arya motioned for me to take the front of the classroom. I glared at Billy and fought back the urge to pummel his face in. I was once a snot-nosed, pimple-faced teenager, but I didn't care who knew about my poetry. It was my escape. My solace from the dark world I lived in. And the ladies loved it. I grinned. Time to make Billy eat his words.

"She's everything that makes smile.

That makes me cry.

She's given me the greatest gift, something to make my life worthwhile.

Because of her I believe in love
And second chances.
Because of her, I'm still alive
And will cherish her forever
For loving me
When I didn't love myself."

A few girls squealed and professed their love for me. Arya laughed, and Billy slunk down in his chair.

"Ah. Matthews?" Ross stuck his head in the door that was left open.

"Oh! Look, another one!" someone said, the room erupting in teenage-girl giggles.

"Duty calls." He waved at Arya.

"Hey, Ross. Take care of my guy here, will ya?" She leaned in to kiss my cheek, but I was quicker and planted a quick kiss to her lips.

"My God. I want a boyfriend," a girl up front said with a loud sigh.

"I'll be your boyfriend," Billy offered.

"You don't even like poetry. A real man likes poetry," she added with a flip of her hair.

"Miss Danvers?" Billy asked.

"Yes?"

"Any room in your poetry class?" Everyone laughed.

Ross and I headed out to our patrol car.

"What we got?" I buckled myself in.

"Some kids being kids not far from here." He started the car and sped off. "By the way, any time you want to come back here, let me know. I want to tag along."

"Oh yeah?" I looked at him out of the corner of my eye.

"Yeah. Miss Ridgewood. She's hot and a total hardass." Ross gripped the steering wheel.

"Uh, and that's a good thing?" I quirked my eyebrow.

"Damn straight. Those hardass ones are the best to crack. The forever kind of love. The take-no-shit kind of woman." He bit his lip and gyrated his hips. "The love-you-long-time kind of woman."

All I could do was laugh. Arya, she wasn't as hard as Miss Ridgewood, but she stood up for what was right. Even if it hurt. And just like Ross, I admired that in a woman. Even if that meant Arya wouldn't take shit from me. That was exactly what I needed. It was all I wanted from here on out.

CHAPTER SEVEN

Arya

I was going on a date with the man I was already in love with. Seemed silly that I was so nervous, but I was. Parker and my relationship was a whirlwind, filled with drama and falling for each other before we knew what even was happening. Taking a step back killed me, but things had been good. Even better than before, and the thoughts of what we were going to do tonight made me giddy.

"Where is he taking you?" Mona asked as she stood in the door to the bathroom.

"No idea. He won't tell me." I grinned as I put some cream in my hair to tame my curls.

"Hmm. He's gotten rather romantic. Has he always been like that?" Mona said in her usual skeptical voice when it came to Parker.

I shook my head. "Not really. It's like he made a full three-sixty. I'm not complaining though."

"He has a lot to lose now," Mona added. "He needs to step it up before you kick his ass to the curb for good."

"Well, I know I have to step it up and that's actually what I intend to do." Parker brushed past Mona and gave me a kiss, taking my hand.

Mona blushed. "Hi, Parker. Who let you in?"

"Mona, always a pleasure to see you." Parker didn't let go of my hand. "Are you almost ready, love?" He looked down at me and, for the first time, I didn't see the heartache and torment that was usually in his eyes.

There was hope.

"I'm ready." Hand in hand, we walked out of the bathroom.

"Parker, a minute please?" Mona cleared her throat and darted her eyes between us.

"I'll be right back." He kissed the base of my hand and went off with Mona. They turned the corner into the hallway but I could still hear them. Not sure Mona knew, but I wasn't going to tell her. She was like my brother, fiercely protective of me. I was afraid she'd grab Parker by the balls and threaten him.

"Don't hurt her, okay? She has expectations and a dream of what life with you is going to be like."

Let the threats begin.

"I know. And I will deliver those expectations plus some. Right now, it's about getting her to trust me again. I want her to know that even when I was knee-deep in depression, she was everything. She *is* everything.

And we are going to be parents and raise this child in a happy, loving family." I heard Parker sigh. "I may have not been the most diligent boyfriend when I lost Emily but I am working on it. I'm becoming the man she always knew I could be."

"I know you're trying but if you can't hack it—"

Parker interrupted her. "I can and I will. I've gone to war. Seen many people I love die. I survived for a reason and that reason was to love Arya. I know that now. My purpose was beyond what I could see at the time. I was drowning in death but I want to live. For her. For our family."

Goddammit. My eyes were leaking. Parker had always had a way with words. What woman didn't want to hear that the man she adored was solely put on this earth to love her?

"All right. Justin trusts you. I trust you. Just had to say it."

"I know. You all love her. But know I love her too." I brought my hand to my heart as Mona came back into the living room.

"What's wrong?" Mona searched my face, her eyes wide.

When Parker rounded the corner, I gripped his cheeks in my hands and crashed my lips down on his. Pressing my body against his, I felt his need for me, hard and ready. Everything about him and me together was right. How we responded to each other physically, but even how, despite what we had been through,

Parker made me cry tears of joy. Because there was no doubt in my mind that he loved me. And holy hell, did I love him.

"Ahem." Mona cleared her throat.

Reluctantly, we parted, breathless and still gripping each other's arms.

"I love you," I whispered.

"And I love you."

I didn't care what the night held or what plans Parker had for us, because hearing his words, feeling his lips against mine, hands down was the start to the best date ever.

***

We pulled up to a house that wasn't familiar. Parker held my hand the entire ride but he was quiet, his eyes never once leaving the road. I didn't want to press him anymore about where we were going, but he was uneasy. He kept squeezing my hand every so often and I could see beads of sweat gathered on his forehead. I'd never seen him like this before. So nervous and unsure. I couldn't help but wish I knew what was going on so I could help ease his nerves.

Releasing my hand, Parker rubbed his chin and finally turned to face me.

"We're here," he said with a forced smile.

"Okay," I said, trying to match his fake enthusiasm.

He got out of the car and headed to my side. He stopped at my door and took a deep breath before opening it.

"Why thank you." I smiled again and snaked my arm through his.

Silence.

Parker stared straight ahead as we walked toward the front door. Ringing the doorbell, he put his hand over mine and squeezed again. I looked up at him, but his eyes remained straight ahead. He squeezed my hand again but that was it.

Let me help you.

The door opened, and a woman around my age gasped before throwing herself into Parker's arms. Our hands parted.

"Oh. It's been too long." She sniffed as she wept. I stood there trying to figure out who she was and why we were there.

"Lindsay, I'd like you to meet Arya." Parker stepped away and brought me close against him. "Lindsay is Jon's wife." Then it all clicked. Lindsay was Jon's widow. One of Parker's battle buddies and best friends who died in his arms.

"It's a pleasure to meet you." I put out my hand for her to shake and she ignored it, bringing me in for a hug.

"How are you feeling? Parker told me you're expecting! How exciting." She glanced down at my stomach.

"I'm great." I looked up at Parker, who seemed like he was holding his breath. This had to be difficult for him. Based on what he'd said, he hadn't seen Jon's and Cooper's families since the funerals.

"Where are my manners. Come in!" With a wave of her hand, Lindsay motioned us inside.

"Where's Marie?" Parker asked as he took in his surroundings.

"She's running late per usual." Lindsay rolled her eyes.

"Marie is Cooper's wife." Parker placed a quick kiss to my hand as we hovered in the living room. Lindsay kept talking and I glanced around, looking at all the pictures. Parker was in so many of them, dressed fully in uniform, smiling with his arm around who I assumed were Jon and Cooper. Over the fireplace was a folded American flag, and my eyes filled with tears. I couldn't imagine losing a husband so young.

"The kids! They've been waiting for you to come. Let me go get them!" Lindsay ran up the stairs, leaving Parker and me alone.

"That's Jon and Cooper before our first deployment." Parker pointed to one of the pictures I had just looked at.

"You guys look so young. And happy." I smiled and picked up the photo.

"We were. Chasing dreams and trying to get the most action. Little did we know where that would get us." Parker shook his head and took the picture out of my hand, placing it on the table, I opened my mouth to ask him why all of a sudden we were here when he had fought so hard to forget this part of his life. Then I heard the sound of children, and two kids came running down the stairs.

"Uncle Parker!" I watched Parker's face crumple at the sight of these two girls, dressed in their princess dresses with makeup and crowns to match. He knelt and they flew into his arms. He almost fell backward.

"Don't ever leave again, Uncle Parker, okay?" One of the girls said. Lindsay was crying in the corner and Parker… his own tears fell.

"I won't, girls. I promise." He brushed their hair back and held them close. I could only imagine how hard it must have been for Parker to look into these girls' eyes when their father died. It was probably easier to run and try to forget. Yet here he was, reopening these wounds and remembering his past that wasn't always kind. But he was trying to mend fences and relationships. I was seeing glimpses of who Parker was before the loss and pain got hold of him. I was thankful he'd brought me here to show me this part of his life that he so badly wanted to pretend never happened. I'd never be able to take the pain away or make him forget, but sometimes the greatest healing comes from remembering.

CHAPTER EIGHT

Parker

There is no other way to describe how it felt to hold these two little girls in my arms other than heartbreaking and beautiful. I felt parts of myself being put back together while at the same time all the memories of Jon battered me and tore me apart. Tori, the youngest at just four, looked just like him. Amanda, the oldest at almost six, spoke just like him when she told me to never leave again. Jon was so much like that. Honest and abrupt.

Tori and Amanda released their death grips on me and talked a mile a minute about all that I had missed when I was away. I tried to keep up but they were talking over each other. I didn't know who Doc McStuffins was but she was the topic of much of the conversation.

"All right, girls. Go upstairs and wash up for dinner," Lindsay said as she wiped her eyes with a tissue. She handed one to Arya, who was crying too.

"Okay, Momma," they said and started running up the stairs. I stood up and turned to Arya, who smiled at me. I felt a tug on my pants and looked down at Tori.

"Uncle Parker, you're still going to be here, right?" Fighting back my tears, I knelt again and looked Tori in the eyes.

"I'm not going anywhere. We're staying here for dinner."

"But after that. You'll visit us?"

I thought of how to answer her question and how confused they must have been when they not only lost their father but another constant in their life. I was so wound up in my own shit that I didn't think about anyone else, not even these precious girls that were like my own children. "I will be around more. Arya and I both will be." I stood up and took Arya's hand in mine. Her eyes were bloodshot from crying. I felt bad springing this visit on her but I feared that if I told her where we were going, there'd be questions and I wasn't mentally prepared for that. I was barely prepared for seeing Lindsay, Marie, and the girls again.

Tori looked at me with her judging eyes that turned into narrow slits. "Will you come to my school play?" She crossed her arms, her sassy attitude coming out.

"If I'm off from work, I'll be there." I winked.

With a smile, she unfolded her arms and gave me a hug. "Okay!" she said in a sing-song voice, and skipped up the stairs. I let out a laugh.

"I'm sorry about the third degree," Lindsay said.

"They had a tough time losing Jon and didn't know what was going on with you."

"It's to be expected. I can only imagine how confusing everything was for them." I cleared my throat, trying to not let the guilt take me over. I've spent the last years of my life fighting the guilt of surviving. The guilt of walking away from Lindsay and Marie when they lost so much too. Even Rainey. I wasn't what she needed when she tried so hard, and now I had to live with the loss of Emily. But there were some things in life that I had no control over and death was one of those things.

"I'm going to finish up with dinner. I want to give you this before. So we can focus on the happy times." Lindsay handed me a small box. "I'll be in the kitchen."

"Let me help you, Lindsay." Arya said as she squeezed my hand. "You okay?"

I kissed her hand. "I will be." With a smile and nod, she followed behind Lindsay.

Opening the box slowly, I nearly dropped it when I saw what it was. Jon's Bronze Star Medal that he received posthumously. I remembered when Lindsay accepted it on his behalf, holding it close to her chest like if she squeezed tight enough it'd bring him back. Why was she giving this to me? I unfolded a letter that was underneath it and read.

I can't be in the room when you open this. I'm taking the coward's way out and writing to you to convince you to take the damn medal and shut your mouth. You, Parker, were the brother Jon never had. The uncle to our daughters, a friend to me. I know you tried so hard to save him and I love you for that. I've had this ready to give to you since that day I received it. You deserve to have this, as a reminder of your heroism and brotherhood with Jon. Remember the good times, let go of the bad. The girls and I would love for you and Arya to be a part of our life, as much or as little as you want. You never stopped being our family, and Jon would want us to continue to be such.

Love, Lindsay, Amanda, and Tori

I didn't realize I was crying until my tears hit the paper. Clutching the letter in my hand and the medal in the other, I ran out the front door and into the yard. I needed to take a breath before dinner. To let myself feel Jon's loss and not stifle it and be thankful for this gift that Lindsay has given me.

Sitting in the grass, I looked around to make sure no one was around. Closing my eyes, I spoke.

"Jon, I'm not sure if you're up there or can even hear me, but I'm sorry. I'm so sorry that I couldn't save your life that day. I left your girls all alone and screwed up so much. I'm here now and going to make up for all the shit I've done. I'll take care of them. Make sure those girls grow up with their uncle Parker." Opening my eyes, I gripped the grass and pulled out a few stalks. "I'm not you. I won't be able to replace what you could have given them, but I will love them. Arya will too. I promise you this, buddy. I won't let you down again."

"Am I interrupting?" Glancing up, I saw Marie smiling down at me. Without waiting for me to respond, she sat down.

We both stared up at the sky, not saying anything. The silence was okay. Almost needed. Marie wasn't as forgiving as Lindsay. I had gotten many angry texts and voice mails from her after I disappeared and signed up for every deployment I could. Lindsay, she understood. Marie, while she knew why I did what I did, was grieving just like I was. Marie and I were a lot alike. We got angry when we were sad and wanted to punch someone or hurt them with our words instead of trying to see their side of things.

"Finally decided to come back around after all this time?" Marie didn't look at me. She stretched her legs out in front of her and sighed.

"It was time."

Marie chuckled. "It was time when Jon and Cooper died and Lindsay and I were trying to pick up the pieces of our lives. You were all we had left of them. The last person to see our husbands alive. Did you ever think that we needed you, Parker?" Marie turned to face me, the anger apparent in her reddened cheeks.

"No. I didn't. I was in a deep, dark place. It's no excuse but I let my mind go. My marriage failed. It was easier to fall apart than to go on without them. And you and Lindsay? You were both just a reminder of all that they left behind. I felt so guilty." I rubbed my face.

"We never blamed you. Ever. When I lost the baby—"

"Wait, you lost the baby?" I jumped up off the ground. Marie simply nodded.

"Why didn't you tell me? Or Lindsay? You could have told Rainey?" I paced back and forth. God, she lost so much. How was she able to stand to be in front of me right now without punching me in the face?

"We tried many times to get in contact with you. We were in contact with Rainey but that wasn't something I wanted to share over the phone. She was so concerned about you." Marie stood up and brushed off her pants.

Just when I finally was ready to move on with my life, the shit kept piling up. I didn't know what to do to make amends for my past, but I had to try. For Jon and Cooper. For myself. I had to let go of my guilt in order to live.

I gripped Marie's shoulders and looked into her eyes. "I'm sorry for not being there. I can't imagine losing your husband and your child."

"It was a boy. I named him Cooper Jr. He's buried next to his father." Marie brushed a tear away.

"They're together," I said. I wasn't the religious type but I believed in something. A higher power that looked down on all of us. And when we died, I'd like to think we were all together with our loved ones. So Cooper was with his son. Marie frowned and brushed my hands off her shoulders.

"Don't think that suddenly we are going to be chummy again. I'm still mad at you." She nudged me with her elbow. "And I'm going to make you work extra hard to be my friend again."

"I wouldn't expect anything less." I grinned.

"Dinner!" Arya called from the front door. I turned to walk inside and Marie gripped my arm and pulled me close against her. I loosened up as we embraced.

"I missed you. You're a damn pain in my ass. Just like Cooper was." She hugged me tighter.

"I missed you too." More than she even knew. Everything wasn't perfect or going to be easy, but things were finally starting to look up and maybe, just maybe, surrounded by all the people I loved, I could be happy and the memory of Jon and Cooper could live on and I could be a part of it.

CHAPTER NINE

Arya

This date wasn't what I expected it to be at all. It was so much more. There weren't flowers or a candlelight dinner, there were emotions and healing for Parker that was far greater than any gifts or romantic meal. This was what I envisioned when I told him I wanted more than his words. While words were beautiful and heartfelt, actions spoke louder. And action was what I received tonight. In all honesty, it's what I'd received every day since I walked out on Parker.

"Can we go back to the apartment?" I shuffled in the seat, my desire for Parker dripping down my legs. This pregnancy already was bringing me cravings and small bits of morning sickness, but my libido? Yeah, that was sky-high.

Parker glanced over at me from the driver seat as he waited for the light to turn green.

"You sure?" he asked, uncertainty lacing his voice.

I took his free hand and moved it up my skirt, groaning with pleasure as I felt his warm fingers brush against my bare skin, stopping at my center. I gyrated my hips. I wanted to be as close to him as possible. To feel every ounce of his body on mine. The weight of him always brought me comfort, warmth, and stability.

"Feel that? That's a fraction of what's going on inside of my body right now. I want you so bad my pussy is aching." I let his hand go. Parker gently moved my panties aside and dipped a finger inside. His eyes widened.

"More. I need more," I begged.

"Fuck," Parker ground out. "Yes. The apartment." A horn sounded behind us. The light had turned green and clearly, we weren't paying attention.

As he drove with one hand, Parker teased my clit with the other. Every neuron in my body fired, the sensation sending my head back against the seat of the car. I wasn't going to last long but I didn't care. I had been waiting since he showed up at the doctor's appointment to do this.

"Don't stop," I said, my voice barely audible. Parker didn't stop, he continued, the sweet, wet sounds of my need for him filling the once silent car.

"Come for me, love," Parker said as he rubbed my clit with his thumb. He slid two fingers in and out, painstakingly slowly, but my God it felt so good.

I gripped the side of the car door and screamed his name before coming all over Parker's hand.

"Fuck me," I said, my head lolling forward. My vision was blurry and my legs felt like Jell-O. My body was coming down from a high, a drug so addictive that I craved more and wanted it as soon as it was over. Parker did that to me. Made me long for him even moments after we were done. He was my drug and there was no cure. Just more and more until there wasn't anything left of me but putty in his hands. But I knew now that his hands were something to treasure and worship, because with just his two fingers he made me scream his name. I wanted that every day. Forever. No, forever and a day, because forever just didn't seem long enough.

"I will," Parker said with a sly smile as he licked each and every one of his fingers.

"You better," I teased. Resting my head against the cool glass of the window, I stared out at the passing cars as we made our way to the apartment. I tried my best to keep my raging hormones under control before I did something crazy like straddle him while he was driving and screw him senseless.

***

Walking into the apartment that Parker and I had shared made me miss seeing his face every morning and kissing him good night. But I was here now and didn't want to dwell on the choices that we both had made. Our future was all that mattered. Together as a family. And once we were living together again, we would be stronger than before.

"Home sweet home." Parker threw his keys in the basket on the side table and rubbed his face. It was his signature move when something was bothering him or he was nervous.

"Hey, why so glum. You're about to get some." I chuckled at my rhyme as I snuggled into him.

"I'm nervous," he muttered.

"For what?" I glanced up at him. It wasn't like we hadn't had sex before.

"The baby."

"Uh, we have plenty of time to figure out this whole parenting thing." I fused myself closer to him.

"No. Not that. But if we have sex is my dick going to bang the baby in the head?" Parker's face turned a shade of pink and I clutched my chest, laughing uncontrollably.

"That's fine. Just laugh it up! I don't know these things." He huffed and fell onto the couch.

"Oh, that's funny." I stopped laughing and straddled Parker. "Listen, sex is perfectly okay during pregnancy. In fact, it's encouraged." Kissing his neck, I gripped his hardness in my hand and give it a gentle squeeze.

"Is that so?"

"Ahum. Doctor's orders. Lots of sex for cardio. And prenatal vitamins for healthy baby and momma."

Slinking down, I knelt before Parker and unzipped his fly. I opened the hole in his boxer briefs, and his dick sprang out.

"He's happy to see you. He's crying tears of joy," Parker said as we both stared down at his precum-covered dick.

"I bet he isn't as happy to see me as I am him." Licking from top to bottom, I devoured his dick. He fisted my hair and pushed me further down against his length. I gagged.

"You good?" he asked through clenched teeth.

"Absolutely." I looked up at him and smiled. I continued working him with my mouth, showing Parker just how much I missed him.

"Fuck. I'm coming." Parker tensed before his body relaxed and he filled my mouth with cum. I swallowed the saltiness, rocking back on my knees.

Parker stared down at me, the most contented smile on his face.

"What?" I asked as I patted down my hair.

"You're beautiful." Parker joined me on the floor and took my face in his hands. "I'm a lucky man. You're amazing for putting up with all of my shit and not running for the hills."

"Well, I did run." I took Parker's hands off my face.

"No, you woke me up to what's important, and that's you and our child." Leaning in, Parker kissed my lips. "I love you," he whispered against them.

"I love you more."

"Not possible, Arya Danvers. You gave me a reason to survive when all I wanted to do was die."

Parker helped me to my feet and guided me to our bedroom. The rest of the night, we spent in each other's arms, showing each other with our bodies how much we truly loved each other. And based on the amount of times I orgasmed, it was enough to last me a lifetime.

CHAPTER TEN

Parker

I've been dreading this day since Arya packed up and left and I knew I had to get my shit together.

Therapy.

David knew his shit, it wasn't that. It was just that opening up and having to share all my fuckups and putting it all out in the open made me uneasy. It all became real once I said what I was considering. If Arya hadn't walked in on me counting those pills and laying them all out like they were a goddamn buffet, I wouldn't be here, and that was tough to wrap my brain around.

I'd wanted to kill myself. To end the suffering of my mind and my past that haunted me. It was a coward's way out, I know that now, but at the time, nothing made sense and to just let it all go? That seemed easier than sitting on this damn couch talking about my feelings.

"So, you screwed up big-time." David leaned back

in his chair and shook his head. "I thought you were doing well, but I understand that losing your sister had to have been difficult."

I snickered. "Difficult? Getting a paper cut can be difficult. Those suckers are a bitch and painful as hell. No, losing my sister ripped me apart and took the little bit of self I had left and tore it to shreds."

"And what did you do?"

I sighed and leaned forward, putting my face in my hands. "I wanted to die. I even lined up the pills. If Arya hadn't walked in on me—"

"You wouldn't be sitting here or preparing for your first child."

"I wouldn't." Releasing my face from my hands, I looked at David.

"It concerns me that this was something that could have happened. Suicidal thoughts aren't something that as a professional I can take lightly. I think you may need medication."

I shook my head. "Absolutely not. I don't want to be a zombie."

"Medication has made many strides. It may take a while to stabilize you and find something that works, but it can be beneficial."

"No. I'm a cop. I need all my faculties about me." I clenched my fists. "Anything else. Aren't there new methods? Virtual therapy or something to help with PTSD?"

David tapped his pen and stayed quiet for a few minutes.

"There is, but there aren't any around here and most of them require inpatient stays."

Fuck. I didn't want to go inpatient. That'd be more time away from work and Arya. But medication? That wasn't an option.

"I can arrange it. Easily. Especially with your diagnosis and attempt at suicide. It's rigorous and can be mentally trying."

I wanted to get better. No medication. I'd do whatever I needed to.

"Let's do it." I sighed and leaned into the couch. I wasn't sure how Arya was going to take the news but it had to be done. I wanted to get better and this was the only way I felt comfortable. In the hands of professionals, exposing myself to the trauma that sent me over the edge and threatened to take all of me, not stifling my feelings and symptoms with medication. I wanted to learn how to cope with my problems on my own. To learn techniques and ways to manage my PTSD. This was going to work. It had to, because I was fucking out of options and time.

***

Arya was busy cleaning up from dinner and I was trying to find the best way to tell her that I was leaving. Things had been going so well. The thought of leaving her and the baby for at least thirty days wasn't something I was looking forward to, but in the end, I knew it was what I had to do.

"We should talk about me moving back in. I'm getting further along in the pregnancy and things are going great. Don't you think?" She turned to me, her face lit up with excitement.

"Arya, I need to go away for a while." Okay, so probably not the best way to tell her. I was an idiot.

"What?" She placed the dish towel on the counter. "Why?"

"I'm checking myself into inpatient therapy in Virginia. David and I think it's the best option. No medication. Intense treatment. Virtual therapy. Daily counseling sessions. It will help me battle my PTSD."

"But you're doing so much better." She rubbed her hands on her pants, leaving behind wet smudges.

"I am. But the fact is that just a month ago I was going to kill myself. That isn't something that will go away overnight. I don't want medication to cloud my mind, or to be dependent on it for the rest of my life. So this is the only other option."

"Wow. I was excited about moving in together again, setting up for the baby, and you're going to go to Virginia." Arya looked away for a moment. "This sucks, but I understand."

I let out my breath that I hadn't known I was holding. "You understand?"

Arya reached out and took my hands in hers. "I do.

It's going to suck to be without you but I'll survive. Maybe I'll take up prenatal yoga or something."

I pulled her into my lap. "That'll make you flexible."

She giggled. "Always thinking about sex." She shimmed her butt against me.

"Damn straight. Your boobs are getting bigger, I think." I gripped them. "Yup, they were always a handful. Now they're more." I leaned down so my face was close to her stomach. "Thank you, baby," I said to the baby.

"You did not just thank our child for making my boobs bigger." Arya rolled her eyes and hopped off my lap.

"Sure did." I grinned. She put her hands on her hips and scolded me.

Something in her shifted, and Arya's face softened. "When do you leave?"

"In a week. It would have been sooner, but I had to make arrangements at work."

"How about I come stay here for the week? So we can spend as much time together as possible?"

"That's a great idea." I stared at her boobs that seemed like they were getting bigger by the minute. I'd swear my mouth was watering.

"Eyes up here, Parker." Arya chuckled.

"I can't help it. I want them in my mouth. Or my hands. Or rubbing against my chest. I'm not a picky man." I shrugged.

"Parker!" Arya screeched as I moved toward her,

licking my lips.

"I'll be gone for a month. I need boobs or I won't survive." I pouted.

Slowly, Arya took off her shirt, a black lace bra underneath. "You need them?" She unsnapped her bra, sending it falling to ground. Her round, full breasts were free, her brown nipples hard and waiting to be licked. "Come and get them."

"Don't challenge me, Arya Danvers. You'll lose." Bending over, I licked her hard nipple, resulting in the most glorious moan from deep within her.

"Game on. Betcha you'll come first."

I grinned. "Challenge accepted."

Fuck. I came first, all over her tits. But I didn't care because I won the day she forgave me and took me back. And no matter what else I did in my life, how inpatient therapy panned out, I knew I'd done something right by falling in love with Arya and fighting for her. Because she was worth it. She was worth everything.

CHAPTER TEN

Arya

Thirty whole days without Parker. Apparently, there was some visitation allowed but from my own experience, I knew it wouldn't be the same. When I was in rehab for my drinking and learning to cope with my rape it was difficult to see my parents and brother. I was so focused on getting better, missing them seemed to set me back. So I denied visitation, and I think I was better for it.

"What are you thinking about?" Parker held my hand as we walked through the neighborhood. I wanted to stay as active as possible, so Parker and I had started walking. It was a nice way to get my exercise in without too much stress or having to go to the gym.

"Just thinking of how you're leaving tomorrow."

"It'll go by quick. And just think, I'll come home as a new and improved Parker Matthews." He gripped my hand tighter.

Maybe I was being paranoid, but part of me was fearful that Parker would change. That he would realize this life that he hadn't planned wasn't what he wanted anymore. He'd been on the fence about having children, and here he was going to be a father. I generally wasn't an insecure person but when you loved someone, the doubts seemed to come with the territory. Every fear came to the surface, and worrying was a common occurrence.

"Nothing is going to change between us. If anything, our relationship will be stronger. Got it?" Parker stopped and looked me in the eyes.

"How'd you know what I was thinking?" I questioned.

"You get this look when you're focused on something." He scrunched his eyes together and made a weird shape with his mouth.

"Stop! I don't look like that!" I swatted his arm.

"It was a lucky guess." He chuckled, his face returning to normal.

Glancing to the side, I realized where we were.

"I used to love this house. I dreamed of living here and decorating all the windows with candles at Christmastime. Isn't it beautiful?" The house was traditional in its colonial style and had tons of windows. It didn't have a white picket fence or any of that other clichéd stuff, it just looked homey. Comfortable, and like it was made for me.

"Oh yeah? Look, it's for sale," Parker said as he

pointed to the sign.

"Yeah. I'm sure it's more than I can afford. I am only a measly schoolteacher." That was the problem with owning a home. With my salary, it wouldn't be possible.

"What about both of us? Together we could afford it," Parker suggested.

I studied Parker to see if he was serious. He was leaving for thirty days and here he was dropping a bombshell on me like buying a house? Together?

"Are you serious?" I tried to maintain my composure but it was difficult. My legs shuffled from side to side and I wanted to jump up and down.

Parker laughed. "Definitely serious."

A car pulled up in front of the house and the real estate agent pictured on the sign jumped out.

"Parker? Arya?" She grinned as her heels clicked against the side walk. "I'm Ginger. You ready to see this beauty?"

I stared at Parker, whose grin hadn't left his face since Ginger stepped out of the car.

"How'd you know?" I whispered. I thought that if my voice was quiet I wouldn't burst into tears, but my God did I want to. Parker constantly amazed me with his generosity and how much he cared about things I liked and didn't like.

"Your parents told me. I wanted to start looking at houses and your mother told me about this place that you always admired. I figured it wouldn't hurt to look at it." Ginger was waiting in the doorway as we spoke.

"I don't know what to say." I rubbed my eyes to make sure I wasn't dreaming.

"Don't say anything. Take my hand and let's hope the inside is all you've ever dreamed, love." Parker took my hand in his and brushed a kiss on top.

"I can do that." Hand in hand we stepped over the threshold. The house was much larger than anything that Parker and I needed now. There were four bedrooms and two and a half bathrooms. But it was beautiful. A new kitchen, a fireplace, and even a huge fenced-in backyard where our child could play. Everything was updated but the old-fashioned colonial charm remained. I didn't say much as we looked in each room. I took it all in, but the feeling…. I knew I was home.

"Well, I'll leave you two to chat about the house. There are already a few people interested. It'll go fast. Prime location. Beautiful. Perfect for a growing family like yours." Ginger stepped outside, her cell phone already attached to her ear.

"What do you think?" Parker leaned against the island in the kitchen and I couldn't help but picture our life here. Me cooking dinner as he sat and told me about his day. A dog running around at my feet looking for scraps, and our child toddling around. It was happiness. A vision of a life that I had only in my dreams. Now, if it could only be a reality.

"I love it, but…."

"But what?" Parker scrunched his face.

"It's big. Four bedrooms? The cost?"

"One, the cost is investing in our future. It's just a little bit more than what we pay for the apartment. And I get the VA loan. No money down. Low interest. Two, four bedrooms are needed for all our future kids. And a guest room." He nodded like what he said was a fact.

"Kids?"

"Of course." Pushing himself off the island, he closed the distance between us. "We can't just have one. They need a brother or sister. They deserve a relationship like you have with Justin. Like I had with Emily." Parker brushed my hair out of my face and cupped my cheeks in his hands. "So, let me ask you again. What do you think?"

"I love it," I said confidently. Chastely, I kissed his mouth.

"Then we'll put in an offer today, before I leave. You will have to handle everything else while I'm gone, but—"

I cut him off with a squeal and wrapped my arms around his neck. He lifted me off the ground.

"Thank you," I said as he held me tightly.

"For what?" Parker placed me down.

"For coming back to me. For trying so hard and making me happy. I think we are going to have a good life together." I heard the front door open and the sound of Ginger's heels.

"No thinking about it, Arya, we are going to have a

great life."

"Well, from the screech I heard outside I think someone might have made a decision?" Ginger smiled wide.

Parker and I looked at each other and I nodded.

"We'd like to put in an offer," I said confidently.

"Excellent!" Ginger started talking fast and pulling out all sorts of paperwork. She'd come prepared, and something in me knew that Parker had already expected to put in an offer. I was sad to see him go, but buying a house would be a distraction from worrying and missing him. I watched as Parker listened intently; the man who a month ago was willing to give up on life, stood here willing to sign on the dotted line to commit to something for the future. It may not have seemed like something major to some, but to me, it was everything.

CHAPTER ELEVEN

Parker

Nothing is ever quite as it seems. I thought I'd hate having to go inpatient for treatment, and while it was an inconvenience for my life, the treatment, the people, they all were like me. When suffering from any mental illness, part of me felt like I was alone, that no one on the face of the earth had ever been through what I was going through. At least not to my extent. That couldn't be further from the truth. In the end, this was where I was supposed to be, surrounded by other veterans who were suffering from PTSD. People who had been to war. Lost brothers-in-arms. People who thought about suicide. I was never made to feel shitty about my choices. They all made sense, and that validated something inside me that I hadn't known I needed.

I wasn't alone. Suffering in silence only harmed me and the ones I loved. For once in my life I made a right choice in coming here.

"Are you ready for your first virtual reality session?" Mary, one of my therapists, asked. I wasn't going to lie, I was fucking scared. I had spent the past week gearing up for this day. There was a lot of prep work involved before the doctors felt comfortable enough to allow me into one of these sessions. It was one thing to replay what happened that day in my mind, it was another to see it in front of me.

"I'm not sure ready is the right word." I followed her down the long, narrow hallway. It was all white, and made me slightly uneasy. There were no pictures lining the walls or clocks hanging to tell me what time it was. Just blank. Empty.

She stopped at a closed door and turned to me. "What would you say is the right word?"

"I know I've been given the tools to be successful, but I'm nervous I guess." I shrugged. Everything here was questioned and analyzed. I felt so exposed 24-7. I couldn't ask for extra mashed potatoes at dinner without being asked why. Like mashed potatoes held the secrets to me managing my PTSD. But it was true, and a valuable lesson. Everything I did in life after Jon and Cooper died had a ripple effect. One bad choice became twenty. I had spiraled and couldn't even see it.

"Being nervous is expected, but remember you're in excellent hands." She smiled and opened the door. The machine was in the center and looked like any normal virtual reality station you would see at the arcade. My nerves settled a bit. I was good at video games, after all.

"Why are you smiling?" Mary asked as she started setting things up.

"It looks like a video game." Mary put the virtual reality glasses over my head as I focused on my breathing. I was trying to focus on anything but what was about to happen. It wouldn't hurt, not in the physical sense, but mentally, I wasn't sure I was ready to come face-to-face with what had happened.

"Now, remember, it's not real, okay?" Mary reminded me. "First we're going to start with some images from your past and move on from there, okay?"

I nodded as a scene came into focus. It was Jon and Cooper, smiling and laughing with their arms around each other. I heard my voice, and they all started laughing. This was when things were so different. Rainey and I were happy. Jon and Cooper were with their families and not thinking about how just a few months later their lives would end.

Everything was different now. They were gone. Jon's children were fatherless. Marie had lost their child. Life didn't turn out how we thought it would. I started to breathe heavy and began to feel overheated.

I reminded myself of what Mary said. This wasn't real, but my God, did I want it to be. I wanted to grab them both and drag them through the screen and have them next to me. I reached out for them, and the scene changed and we were on patrol. My heart clenched and I knew this was when all hell broke loose. It was different going through it a second time.

Shit. Who was I kidding? I'd been through this a million times in my mind. Where I stepped. How quick my reaction time was after Jon was shot. It was never right. I never did enough. I wasn't quick enough. I didn't step carefully enough.

It was odd being in virtual reality because it all seemed so real. I could almost feel the sand underneath my boots, crunching as I glanced all around me. Even the blazing sun I swear I could feel kissing my skin. Then it happened, gunshots, screaming. I expected I would freeze when faced with this situation again, but I didn't. I tried to save the lives that were being taken just like I did the first time and Jon was standing next to me. Leaning down next to this man who I didn't know, I tried to cover the wound on his neck. I lifted my hands in front of my face and saw blood dripping from them. Looking into this man's eyes again it was like looking into Jon's. I watched his life start to leave his body. His breathing staggered. His body became limp. This time, I held his hand.

"I don't want you to go but I know you have to." I gripped his hand tighter. "I'm going to finish up this treatment program and make you and Cooper proud. I'll be the best damn cop and father I can be." The man smiled, and everything went black.

It was easy for me to associate this scene with the loss of Jon. There were so many similarities and while I expected to crumble, struggle and beg him to stay, I didn't. Because no matter what, at the end of the day,

Jon and Cooper were gone.

I ripped off the headset, my chest heaving with my breaths.

I stumbled back against the wall, thankful to have it to prop myself up.

"How do you feel?" Mary asked. The dreaded question. I didn't feel anger. That was what I was accustomed to. I wasn't thinking that I didn't do enough. That somehow, someway, I should have known what was going to happen to Jon and Cooper and protected them. My brain knew now it wasn't a possibility. All I could do moving forward was honor their memory.

"I feel like I'm going to be okay." Mary grinned and patted my arm.

"Well, Parker. I think you may be right."

I was right because I had everything to live for. It's hard when your mind fought against your innate instincts of survival. That's what having PTSD and depression was like. Your survival instincts were still there but they're skewed. Masked by the pain, loss, and despair. Part of me wanted to get up and go on, so I did that, but I hated it. Resented that Jon and Cooper weren't there. It was chaos in my own mind and body.

Things could change, though. Life could kick you in the ass, bring you to your knees, but then, it all stopped. The migraines ended. The loss wasn't as poignant, and it all was because of love. Love for a child. Love for a woman who had her own demons and kicked their asses. More importantly, love for myself and realizing that I could make mistakes. Royally shitty mistakes, but I could overcome them and maybe even find happiness in the face of loss and sadness.

I, Parker Matthews, was going to be okay.

CHAPTER TWELVE

Arya

It'd been two weeks since I'd seen Parker. It wasn't easy having him away but dealing with all the paperwork, inspections, and picking out paint colors for the house kept me busy. But today, I wanted him here with me more than any other day since he left. My hormones were all crazy. One day I hated him for being away, even though it was for a perfectly valid reason. Another day I liked my alone time and walked around the house with my growing belly on display in just my underwear and bra after an hour-long walk. Then I ate a carton of ice cream. It was all about balance.

Today I cried and cried. Today was the day we found out the sex of the baby, and Parker wouldn't be here. My mother wanted to come with me. Mona sat in my car, refusing to get out, and tried to get Justin to convince me to let her come with me. I appreciated everyone wanting to come and be with me but no one could replace Parker. Not that they were trying to, but this was something I wanted reserved for only us. A special moment that we would share together. Whenever that might be.

"Okay! Let's check on everything and find out what you're having." The ultrasound technician lifted up my shirt and put the gel on my stomach.

"There's the head." The tech kept talking, but my mind was elsewhere. I couldn't shake the fact that I didn't want to find out the gender of our baby without Parker here, regardless of how anxious I was to know. Was I carrying a precious girl who would wrap Parker around her finger? Or was it a boy who would be so much like Parker that I'd be the one whipped.

"Actually," I sat up and pulled my shirt down, "if you could just put the gender in an envelope, I'd like to wait to find out."

"Oh. Sure." She smiled politely and jotted down the information on a piece of paper and put it in an envelope. "Everything looks great. The baby is healthy and growing perfectly."

"That's great. I'm sorry to be such a pain. I thought I wanted to know, but with Parker not here it doesn't seem right." I rubbed my stomach as the baby moved in agreement.

"I get it. You should do a baby shower and reveal the gender. That's all the rage now."

"That's actually not a bad idea. I'm sure my mother is planning some sort of baby shower that will put the royal wedding to shame." We both laughed.

She helped me off the table. "Whatever you decide, it'll be great."

It would be, because whether a boy or girl, a huge party or a small celebration with my family and friends, this baby was a blessing and I'd spend the rest of my life counting my lucky stars. My life may not have been perfect, it may have had its disasters, but in the end, I knew there'd be a point where I could smile and say, "It was all worth it."

****

I pulled down my dress for the hundredth time and stared at the door as everyone else but Parker seemed to come through. It always amazed me how people with mental illness all looked normal. There were no bruises or scars on the outside that I could see and easily distinguish that they were ill. Their burdens were carried deep within them, and that was worse. No one knew that they were struggling. Getting help could be difficult because they had to ask. I remembered it all like it was yesterday, struggling with my drinking and severe depression. No one knew. I went about my life like nothing was wrong when at just eighteen years old I drank to excess to escape.

My body stilled when I saw him, the man who

had quickly become my life. I never thought I'd meet someone like Parker, who understood me deep down to my soul. He wasn't perfect but that wasn't what I wanted. I wanted him with all his challenges because with those came his sense of humor, his sensual side. The good came with the bad and that was okay because we were a team. And our "bads" complemented each other. We understood the struggles and challenges that went with recovering from mental illness, and we knew that we were stronger together. It just took us a bit to realize it.

"Arya." Parker smiled and glanced down at my stomach, which had grown a bit in the last few weeks. He placed his hands gently on my stomach and rubbed. "You look beautiful." He leaned in and kissed me; it was quick, much quicker than I wanted, but given that we were in a room with many other people, I understood. But damn did I want more.

"You look good yourself." I tugged on the hem of his shirt. He put his arms around me, and I leaned against his chest. "I miss you. A lot." I sighed as I breathed in heavily, the scent of him calming me. All my worries, emotions, everything seemed to still. Parker was my serenity.

God how I love this man.

"I miss you too. I'm almost done. It's been good, though. Really good." Parker smiled down at me before leading me to an empty table in the corner.

I sat next to him and he took my hand, the smile

never leaving his face. He seemed happy, despite being here and away from his job and family. It was good to see him this way when the alternative was too difficult to fathom. A life without Parker in it.

"What are you thinking about?" Parker asked as he kissed my hand.

"You look happy, and what the alternative would have been if you didn't decide to get help." Tears pressed against my eyes. "A life without you…."

"Hey. None of that." Parker leaned in and brushed my tears away. "I promise I am doing everything I need to never get to that point again."

"Good." I shimmied closer to him. "Because I'm super needy 24-7 and my battery-operated boyfriend isn't cutting it anymore. You need to come home." I winked and linked my arm through his. I looked into his eyes that had turned dark. Licking his lips, he brushed back my hair.

"Open your legs, Arya," Parker said, his voice turning to a deep growl. I felt it all the way down to my core. In my center that pulsed with desire for him.

His fingers brushed against my bare legs, slowly tracing circles as they snuck up my dress.

"Parker, someone might see."

He smiled before dipping one finger inside my wet folds. I held back my moan.

"Better be quiet then, love." He kissed the tip of my nose.

"Please…," I begged as silently as possible as

he added another finger. They dipped in and out painstakingly slowly. I wanted nothing more than press myself against him and beg for mercy, but I couldn't. His thumb teased my clit and I knew I was close. Goose bumps travelled over my skin and I gripped the end of the table, my release taking me over.

"Is she okay?" I sat up straighter as a woman came to stand across from us.

"Oh. Yes, she's fine. Just a little hungry, right?" Parker nudged me and I nodded, because quite honestly that's all I could do. If I opened my mouth I would scream Parker's name and demand he pull out his dick.

Classy, I know.

"Here!" She reached into her purse and pulled out a cookie. She blew on it and I watched the dust fly off. She handed it to me.

"Thank you," I managed to say. Parker rubbed his mouth and I knew he was trying to hold it together.

"You're welcome. I have a few more in here somewhere." She rifled through her bag.

"No, thank you. One is plenty." I held the cookie in my hand and she stood, not moving.

"I think she wants you to take a bite," Parker whispered.

"It's a purse cookie," I said as quietly as possible. A purse cookie with dust.

"Pretend," he added.

Acting like I was taking a bite, I chewed as convincingly as possible.

"All right then! See you later!" She bounced away and back over to the people she was visiting.

Parker and I looked at each other and busted out laughing.

"That was interesting." He said as he grabbed my hand again. He placed his other hand on my stomach.

"It was." We looked into each other's eyes and smiled. For the first time there were no barriers, no thoughts of what-if, just us and a life that didn't seem half that bad.

CHAPTER THIRTEEN

Parker

I walked down the hallway that had been my constant for the past month. The same white walls, the sounds of people milling about and trying to find some peace when all they'd had was struggle and loss. It was a feeling I was familiar with. So many of these people I was able to relate to. I wasn't alone.

Today was my last appointment with the therapist. Next I would be sent home to start my life. To move into my home with Arya and try to find routine, normalcy, and happiness.

Those were all things I had before, but by being here I realized that timing sometimes doesn't work in our favor. Rainey and I married so young, and while my love for her will always be there, it changed over time. She became the person I let down, but she also became the person who pushed me harder than anyone else. For the way she loved me, encouraged me, pushed me toward success, I'll be forever grateful. I cheated on her, pushed her away because in my mind I was broken. In a way I was, I think I always will be, but as I fought to put myself back together, I knew out of all the things I'd done in my life, the fucked-up shit and sometimes noble things, letting Rainey go was the best choice for not just her but myself. When we were young, we needed each other, fed off each other's love and couldn't survive without it. I realized that love shouldn't be about survival, it should be about want. A desire so strong that while you knew you might be able to live without the person, the thought wasn't fathomable. Arya was that for me. At that point in my life, I was ready for forever. To settle down with Arya and welcome children into our lives. Was I scared? Damn straight. I was fucking petrified, but I was ready, where before I couldn't even get out of my own way.

I opened the door to the office and saw David sitting next to my therapist, Anne. He smiled and stood up, taking me into a quick hug.

Why is he here?

"Why are you here?" I asked.

"I wouldn't miss this for the world. I know we haven't always seen eye to eye on everything but I've always been invested in your healing." David smiled as he looked me up and down. "You look good, Parker." He took his seat. I rubbed my eyes. Damn. There were so many people that had surrounded me for years that I didn't even know cared. Or I was too blind to see it. It was easier to pretend that I was all alone than to realize I had support. "How's it been? You ready to get out of here?"

I sat across from Anne and David and crossed my legs. I was ready to get out of there and start my life, to finally put the pieces back together. I didn't want to let anyone down. My entire life I'd felt like a failure, one step behind what everyone's expectations were for me. I learned, though, that the only expectations that mattered at the end of the day were the ones I had for myself.

I wanted to be a good father. A good man to Arya. A good cop. I was sure there would be some added over time but for now, baby steps.

"I'm ready. It's been good. Anne and everyone here have been a huge help in helping me figure everything out. I think I have the tools to live a halfway decent life."

Anne sat forward a bit and smiled. "I know you do, Parker. Remember, don't beat yourself up over things that you can't control. You aren't going to not feel guilt ever again, never be scared or frustrated. Just know you have the tools to be successful and to move on. Forward momentum, not backward."

"Forward. Always forward." I thought of the rules of war and how we were taught to push forward regardless of how we felt. Your legs hurt from ruck marching twenty miles? Keep going. You missed your family after being gone for a year? Keep going. I didn't know when "keep going" became so hard for me, but it did. The guilt of it was too much because I wanted to be strong but I couldn't. Being strong came in many different forms. Sometimes being strong meant letting someone know you needed help.

I had finally found my strength. It wasn't in holding a gun, fighting crime, or going off to war, it was in myself. It was buried deep and required a bit of digging around to find it, but it was there and it felt good to be in control again.

"Someone is here for you. David will still be seeing you weekly to track progress. Help with any coping you may need. You have so much to be thankful for." Anne jotted a few notes down on her notepad.

"I survived," I said out loud. David looked at me and nodded. "I used to think my survival was a curse but it wasn't."

"Surviving is never easy. The guilt can be tortuous, but everyone has a purpose. So, my last question for you, Parker, is what's yours?"

I thought about it for a minute. I knew that I made a good cop. It came naturally, like being in the army did, but I realized that wasn't it. There was more to me than a rough and tumble guy.

"To love. Be happy. Be a father. God, I have too much to live for." I smiled and pictured Arya's smiling face and growing belly.

"Well, go love her then," Anne said.

"That's what I intend to do. Every day for the rest of my life."

****

"Hey bud." Justin stood outside the door to the inpatient area, his hands shoved in his pockets. "Arya is going to fucking kill me for not telling her that you're being released today."

I laughed as I signed myself out.

"It's for a good reason. I want to surprise her."

"She'll be surprised all right. She's been moping around our parents' house all day saying how she wished you could be there for the baby shower."

"I'll be there. I need to make a few stops first. You good with that?"

"Hell yah. I told the girls that I had important business to do today for work. I don't want to be around all those women fawning over baby stuff any sooner than I have to be. Mona's going to be all wide-eyed. Her ovaries are going to be popping." He shook his head and rubbed his face. Motioning to the front of his pants, he frowned. "Shut down until further notice. She's like fertile Myrtle."

"Babies aren't that bad." We walked toward Justin's truck. He stopped and stared at me.

"I'll remember you said that when you're up at 1:00 a.m. feeding for the tenth time. And you get peed on or pooped on for the first time. It's all fun and games until vomit makes it into your mouth." Justin shuddered.

"You're a doctor!"

"So? Who wants to be thrown up on? Not me." He unlocked his doors and we piled in.

"Where to first?" he asked.

"The party store."

With a smile, we headed off.

***

I walked into the banquet facility with Justin leading the way.

"She's hormonal. Be careful. She might throw something at you or pass out. It could really go either way."

"It's fine. I'm prepared for anything." I carried the piñata that was stuffed with either blue or pink glitter and confetti. I knew Arya had the sex of the baby in an envelope and was waiting for us to be together to find out, but I wanted it to be special and this was the best I could do with such short notice. Thankfully, Justin managed to sneak a peek at the envelope for me and find out ahead of time.

"I said that too when Mona was pregnant." Justin gripped my shoulder. "You indeed are not ready for everything."

"Oh, my God!" Arya's mother nearly tackled me in

the hallway. "You're here!" She tried to be quiet but her voice was high-pitched and squealy.

"Shh! Don't ruin the surprise," Justin said.

"I am here. Want to let Arya know she has a big surprise?" I peered around the corner and saw her finishing opening up presents.

"I'm telling her. I didn't lug you around all day to not get the credit." Justin walked into the room and I heard him ask everyone to be quiet.

"Hey, everyone. I'm Justin, the big brother of this beautiful lady, for those of you that don't know me. I wanted to get you a good present but looks like you have all you need." He looked around at all the gifts that surrounded her. Our baby was loved. That was for sure. "But I thought of what the next best thing would be. Close your eyes."

Arya complained. "You're going to do something mean. I know it." She crossed her arms.

"Stop complaining and do what I say for once." Everyone laughed. She closed her eyes, and Justin motioned me in. Quietly I walked into the room and knelt in front of her. I was careful not to touch her or make any noise. Everyone started taking pictures and video. I noticed Lindsay and Marie and waved at them. Both were already tearing up and hugging each other.

"Okay. Open," Justin said.

Arya opened her eyes and gasped. She lunged forward and I managed to catch her without falling backward.

"You're here! You're really here." She touched my face, my chest, anything she could get her hands on. Gripping her cheeks, I kissed her, long and hard, not caring who saw it.

"I'm here, love, and I'm not going anywhere ever again."

"Good." She smiled as we stood up. "Just when I thought this day couldn't get any better, you show up. You completed this day for me."

"You completed my life the moment you walked through that classroom door." I kissed her hand.

She blushed. "Want to help me open the rest of these presents?" She wiped the tears off her cheeks.

"Actually, I have another surprise for you." I grinned.

"My heart can't take anything else." She brought her hand over her chest.

"This is for everyone." Her mother came out with the piñata and hung it with Justin's help.

"What's that for?" Arya asked.

"So we can find out what we're having. A boy or a girl. Together, surrounded by all our friends and family."

"How did you pull this off?" She tugged on my shirt.

"Your brother helped. He's not half that bad."

Justin snorted. Arya ran to him and hugged him so tight I thought she was going to suffocate him. "Thank you both. So much. I love you guys."

"We love you too." With Justin on one side of her

and me on the other, things couldn't get much better. I was here, my mind not plagued with my normal anxiety and worries. All I could think about was whether I was having a little boy or girl.

"You ready?" Arya's mother held a stick. "I can't wait much longer!" She jumped around a bit.

Arya took the stick and everyone gathered around.

"Okay, everyone. Stand back. Arya sucked at sports growing up," Justin joked.

The stick hit the piñata and pink glitter and confetti fell all around us.

"It's a girl," I whispered. "We're having a girl!" I said louder. Tears streamed down Arya's face and I grabbed her, bringing her close against my chest.

"Are you ready for this?" she asked through her tears.

"I'm ready. That little girl is going to get whatever she wants. I already love her so much." Bending down, I kissed her stomach.

"Hey baby girl, I love you. And you know what else?" I looked up at Arya, who was smiling down at me. "I love your momma too. More than she'll ever know."

"I know, Parker. I've always known. That's why I never gave up on you. Love has the best healing power. And I'll never stop loving you."

"I'll never stop loving you. Either of you." With one hand still on Arya's stomach, I kissed her. "Now we get to pick out names."

"What do you mean? It's a girl. Her name will be Emily." I took a step back and looked at Arya. I hadn't thought I could love this woman any more, but I did. Arya was a rare woman who loved with all she had.

"Emily." I wept as I held Arya, and people snapped pictures. No one could hear our conversation, but this was one of the best moments of my life. I was going to have a little girl and she was going to have me wrapped around her finger forever. And I wouldn't trade it for the world.

CHAPTER FOURTEEN

Arya

Emily was doing somersaults in my belly. She was getting restless in there and I couldn't blame her. Truth was, I was ready for her to be in my arms. Not to mention, I hadn't seen my feet in weeks or had a decent night's sleep in forever. I was a stomach sleeper, which was a big no-go when I was as pregnant as I was.

I was curled into Parker's side in our new home, finally getting to breathe and relax. Things had been go, go, go since Parker came home. We moved into the house right after he was released. After a few weeks, he went back to work. It was an adjustment for him, but everyone at the police department was super supportive. It was an easier transition than anticipated. Parker was seeing a therapist regularly, working out daily, and seemed happy. I always thought that happiness had to mean that there were no issues. No moments where you felt weak or like shit just wasn't fair. No.

Happiness was life, the good and bad. Because without the bad, I couldn't appreciate something as simple as lying on the couch with the man I loved. Or our child. The unexpected gift that took us both by surprise. Life was full of happiness, sometimes it was just difficult to see through the pain.

It'd been months of adjusting, reconnecting, and getting back into a routine. It wasn't easy being with Parker sometimes. His demons were still there; they always would be, but he was worth it. Our family was worth it. The difference now was that he let me in and shared things about his past. It brought us closer. It made us stronger. And I loved him even more than the first day I met him in my classroom.

With a sigh, I cuddled closer into Parker. He took my hand and kissed it as he remained focused on the TV. We had become obsessed with the show *Stranger Things* and binge-watched it whenever he had free time from work.

Glancing at my feet on the ottoman, I groaned in frustration. They were swollen and looked like Hot Pockets.

"What's wrong?" Parker asked as he searched my face.

"My toenails are hideous. I can't go into labor with my toes looking like cat claws." I attempted to sit up, and with a gentle push from Parker, I made it to my feet. Parker's eyes followed me as I waddled in front of the TV. He smiled and I flipped him off. He loved my body that was growing our child. I was frustrated that I couldn't see my feet. The only plus was that my stomach made a good ice-cream bowl holding spot. I headed into the bathroom and rifled through my cosmetic drawer and pulled out all my nail stuff.

I am going to make my nails pretty. That'd make me feel better.

I plopped myself back on the couch. Leaning over a few times, each time with more force than the last, I realized I couldn't reach my feet. The tears fell—not silently. I sobbed like someone had died. In a way, something did—my ability to reach my goddamn feet!

God, I was ridiculous. I should have known I couldn't paint my toenails. I couldn't even put on my sneakers and tie them without Parker's help.

"Baby." Parker knelt beside the couch and took the polish from my hands. "It's okay."

"I can't reach my feet." I sniffed. "I'm going to have ugly feet when I meet our baby for the first time." I was full-on sobbing again. "My feet are swollen. I can't sleep. I pee every five minutes." I started listing all my frustrations about being so close to going into labor.

"Shhh." Parker gently placed the polish down on the coffee table and stood.

"Come with me." Parker held out his hand.

"What?" I wiped my eyes and placed my hand in his. He helped me off the couch and led me to the door. He helped me slip into my sandals, the only things that my feet would fit in.

"We're going to go to the nail place and you're going to get pampered." Parker handed me my purse.

I smiled. "You mean it?"

"I mean it." Parker smiled back.

"Only if you get a pedicure with me," I joked as we headed to the car.

Parker shook his head as he helped me into the passenger seat.

"I'd do anything for my girls, but pretty sure I'd lose my man card if I got a pedicure."

"It's relaxing. Don't knock it until you try it." Resting my head against the back of the seat, I listened to the music. Parker took my hand in his. Lacing my fingers through his, I relished in the serenity, the normalcy that our life had taken on. Parker was home.

***

"What can I get for you two today?" the receptionist at the desk asked.

"A manicure and pedicure, please," Parker said, his hand resting on the base of my back.

"Excellent, right this way." Parker wiggled his eyebrows as we followed behind her. She led us to pedicure stations where two women waited for us.

"Oh, no. Just her." He smiled politely and helped me into the chair. Taking off my shoes, he placed them beside me.

"Aw, come on, babe. No one will ever know." I giggled.

"Men do it all the time. Your feet will be so nice!" one of the girls said. "It's actually rather sexy when men take care of themselves." A few murmurs of agreement filled the air.

With a reluctant sigh, Parker sat next to me and took off his shoes.

"If you tell any of the guys at the station about this...," Parker warned.

I laughed and closed my eyes as the chair started to vibrate.

"Shit, the chairs massage you?" Parker said loudly. A few chuckles came from around us.

Within a few minutes everything was silent. I opened my eyes and looked beside me and saw that Parker had fallen asleep.

I took out my phone and snapped a picture. It was a memory I never wanted to forget. A snapshot into the real Parker. He struggled with his PTSD. Had been to war too many times to count and suffered so much loss, but at the end of the day, deep down beneath all that pain was a man who would get a pedicure with his pregnant girlfriend just to make her happy. Parker Matthews wasn't perfect, but it was moments like these that made me feel that he was damn close.

CHAPTER FIFTEEN

Parker

When I was younger, I used to wish for a different life. With my stomach grumbling in hunger and praying that I'd wake up and my parents wouldn't be drug addicts, or I'd open the fridge for the third time that night hoping for food, I wanted to be in any other family but the one I was born into. I ran from everything, joined the Army, got married, and promptly ruined it all. I got what I wanted. A new life. A fresh start, but I wasn't ready. I was running, trying to forget, when all I needed to do was remember and face my fears. My failures. My issues.

Now I was ready and facing and owning up to everything wasn't easy. It was worth it because it brought me my girls.

As I stared at Arya as she slept, I realized that everything happened for a reason. Clichéd, yes, but it's true. My life has had its fair share of challenges, loss, even regrets, but the one thing I don't regret is letting love into my life again. Suffering from PTSD is like living in a constant state of questioning. Why me? Why did I live and Jon and Cooper didn't? How could Emily be taken from me when I had already lost so much? I thought love was wasted on me. All that Rainey offered was better suited for someone else. Rainey and I weren't meant to last forever, but love, it didn't see me for my PTSD. It didn't know about my past and raise its eyebrows and turn away, it opened its arms again and gave me not only Arya but a child that I could love and cherish forever.

So again, yes, I thought why me? But not for something bad, for something so precious and pure that I wasn't sure if I deserved it, but fuck, I'd spend the rest of my life proving that I was worthy.

"Arya." Leaning over, I brushed a kiss to her forehead. "I have a surprise for you." She groaned and opened her eyes, shooting daggers at me. Sleep was hard for her to come by lately but I had been waiting for this day for what seemed like forever.

"Parker Matthews, I swear to God if you are showing me something stupid I will kill you. I was having the best nap since I got pregnant."

"Duly noted. It'll be worth it." With a groan, I helped her out of bed. She followed me down the hall muttering under her breath.

We stopped at the nursery door and she crossed her arms.

"Close your eyes."

"Parker, what did you do?" Her eyes were big and wide as she stared at me. I'd spent so much time researching, talking to her mother, Mona, and anyone who would help me to make this nursery fit for a princess.

"Just close your eyes, baby." I wrapped my arms around her and brushed a kiss to her cheek. With a sigh, her eyes shut.

The door creaked open and I guided her inside, stopping right in the middle of the room. I took in my handiwork. The light gray furniture, rocking chair, and rug. There were splashes of pink throughout, not too much because my daughter didn't need to fit some stereotype. She could like blue or green or whatever she wanted; regardless she'd be my princess.

My favorite part of the room were the baby pictures of Arya and me that were hung around. There were so few of me when I was younger; taking pictures and remembering my childhood wasn't the most important thing for my parents, but there were a few and for that I was grateful. My daughter wouldn't know what it was like to be hungry, to question if her parents loved her. Her childhood would be nothing like mine.

"Open your eyes." Arya's eyes shot open and she gasped, bringing her hand to her mouth. She was speechless as she walked around the room, her hand touching and caressing everything. I let her look and take everything in.

"You did all this?" She stopped at the rocking chair and pushed it with her foot, watching it go back and forth.

"I did. I had lots of help though. Is it good? Do you like it? We can change anything...." Arya ran toward me, well as fast as a nine-month-pregnant woman could run, and threw her arms about my neck. She didn't kiss me but held me close, closer than she ever had.

"It's perfect. Beautiful. She's going to be our princess. Our everything."

I grabbed Arya's cheeks and looked into her eyes.

"She already is our everything. Since you told me that night when I was struggling to stay alive. You both are my everything and always will be." Tears streamed down Arya's face, and I brushed them away.

Arya and I both started fussing over all the baby items. Everything was so tiny and cute.

"I love this crib," Arya said. It was round and different than the normal rectangular ones.

"Your mother insisted that Emily needed this fancy crib. Heaven forbid her first granddaughter had anything less." Arya laughed.

"This is amazing, Parker. Now we just need a baby." She rubbed her stomach.

"Well, you know what they say helps get labor started?" I gripped the side of the crib and licked my lips.

"Oh. I know that look. I'm a cow. You can't possibly want to have sex with me."

Releasing the crib, I moved toward Arya and brushed aside her hair. "I'll always want you. But right now, as you grow our child inside your body, I've never wanted you more. Let me make love to you."

Arya giggled.

"What's so funny?" I quirked my eyebrow.

"Make love? Why don't you fuck me, fast and hard?" Arya closed the little bit of distance that was between us and attempted to rub her center against mine. The baby belly certainly got in the way nowadays.

"Now you're speaking my language," I joked.

Lacing our hands together, we walked out of the nursery.

"Hopefully next time we're in here it's with baby Emily," Arya commented.

I sprinkled kisses all down her neck, half listening as my dick got harder and harder.

"Ahum," I murmured against her skin.

"Parker."

"Yes?" I nibbled her ear.

"I think it's time."

"Oh, it's time, baby. I'm going to…." My eyes shot to hers and Arya stood there, holding her stomach as water trickled down her leg. "Shit, are you okay?"

"I'm fine. My water broke. Let's go have a baby."

Needless to say, my priorities shifted. We were going to have a baby. My Emily was ready to enter the world.

CHAPTER SIXTEEN

Arya

I always wanted to be a mother. I dreamed of having a big family and thought often of how glorious being pregnant would be. Even when I was a little girl and I'd play house, I'd stuff my shirt with a pillow and pretend to be pregnant. My dad nearly had a heart attack each time but being a mother was something that I always knew I wanted. I had a wonderful mother. Two great parents, really; being like them is something I aspired to.

Being pregnant wasn't that bad, except until the end when I couldn't see my feet or bend over without feeling like I was going to pass out from lack of oxygen to my brain. Growing a human was no joke. Other women who'd given birth had told me how they felt like they were being torn in two when every contraction hit. That they'd wanted to kill anyone within their line of sight. But most important, they told me how the epidural was a Godsend and to not pass it up, that it would make labor enjoyable.

Enjoyable wasn't really the word that came to mind.

Of course, I'd be the one in back labor. The epidural was shit and could have been half a Tylenol in the grand scheme of things.

"I wish I could take all your pain away." Parker rubbed my back as my mother fussed with my blankets. If she tucked me in one more time I was going to lose my shit.

I smiled as best I could and closed my eyes. I'd been in labor for twelve hours. No progress. It'd take time, the doctor said. Some women were in labor for days, and the way things were going, I was convinced that was going to be me.

Another contraction hit and my eyes shot open. I tried to be strong, but a whimper escaped my lips.

I can do this. I've been through much worse.

"What can I do?" Parker practically climbed into bed with me.

"Ice chips?" I asked as my mom patted my forehead with a cool cloth.

"Coming right up." Parker placed a kiss to my forehead and shot out of the room like my life depended on those ice chips. I loved how attentive he was, his willingness to do anything for me.

My stomach growled in protest. "I'm starving. I could eat like ten burgers right now."

"I know. It'll all be over soon," my mother reassured.

Something in me wasn't so sure. I always tried to be optimistic, but this, being in labor, wasn't hoping that the grocery store carried your favorite ice cream this week, or that the sweater I really loved came in my size; this was bringing life into the world and hoping that everyone made it out healthy and alive.

The door to my room opened and Parker came in with the pink pitcher. He looked tired. Dark circles were under his eyes and I realized I wasn't the only one who was tired and probably hungry. My mother and Parker had been by my side the entire twelve hours without a single break. We all needed to regroup.

"Why don't you and Mom go down and get something to eat?" I said as Parker fed me ice chips.

"No. I'm not leaving. What if something happens when I'm gone?" He shoved more ice chips in my mouth.

"Parker—" The door swung open just as my mother starting speaking.

"Hello." Dr. Sanderson entered and washed her hands quickly. "I'm going to do a quick check and see how things are progressing. If we need a little push, I think we should administer some Pitocin to get the process rolling a bit more."

"I think that'd be great." Parker stood on one side of me and my mother on the other.

"Well, looks like still three centimeters. Definitely time to get things moving quicker. What do you say?" Dr. Sanderson pulled the blanket back over me and patted my leg.

"Let's do it." I looked at Parker just as he squeezed my hand.

"All right, the nurse will be right in with that. It can take a bit, so rest up and maybe you two can go get a bite to eat or something?"

Parker grunted.

"Oh, Parker. Relax. She's going to get the medicine. It'll be a while before it all kicks in. Come have coffee with your future mother-in-law." My mom wrapped her arm around Parker's shoulders.

"Are you sure you're going to be okay?" Parker looked like he was going to be sick at the thought of leaving me.

"I will. I'll take the opportunity to get a bit of rest. Our baby will be here before you know it." Leaning over, he brushed a kiss to my lips.

"I can't wait."

"Me either. Now go get some caffeine. I love you guys."

"We love you too, dear," my mother said as the door closed behind them.

Within a few minutes of them leaving, the nurse came in and started my IV.

"The contractions will start getting closer together and more painful. It can take a bit though, so I recommend resting while you can." She patted my arm.

"Fabulous," I joked.

"If you need anything just use your call button."

The sounds of the machines filled the silence. My eyes started feeling heavy and I was grateful for the momentary peace.

No sooner did I doze off than the alarming sound of loud beeping filled the air. My chest started tightening, and I could barely get any air into my lungs.

Nurses rushed into my room and all I could hear was them talking about how the baby's heart rate was dipping dangerously low and my blood pressure was sky-high.

"Where does it hurt?" the nurse asked.

"My chest," I wheezed out. Everything tightened and I started with a coughing fit.

"We've got to get them both into the OR stat. The baby is crashing. Her blood pressure is too high."

Within seconds I was whisked down the hallway. In that moment, all I wanted was Parker by my side, his reassurance that everything was going to be okay. His kisses on my forehead.

My body started going numb.

"I can't feel anything." The nurse looked down at me and frowned. I saw her lips moving but I couldn't hear anything. I opened my mouth to ask for Parker, but nothing came out. This couldn't be happening. I closed my eyes and said a silent prayer to whoever was listening to spare at least our child. Parker couldn't take another loss, but maybe if the baby survived he could be strong. He had to be. I tried to open my eyes but they wouldn't budge. I was cold, freezing as I tried to stay present. But no matter how hard I tried my body resisted and everything went black.

CHAPTER SEVENTEEN

Parker

My coffee was cold and the hospital sandwich was rock solid. It would be better used as a hockey puck than as sustenance. My mind was anywhere but focused on what Pearl was saying to me. I have no idea how she could be so calm. All I wanted to do was be by Arya's side.

"And just think! If you have any more kids you'll be a pro," Pearl said before taking a sip of her coffee.

My eyes widened as I looked at her. She smiled.

"I want to get through this first birth, please. Then we can talk about more kids." I took a swig of my cold coffee. Although more kids were in our future, seeing Arya in so much pain wasn't pleasant. "Do you think we should go back upstairs?" I glanced at my phone and saw that we'd been gone only twenty minutes.

Pearl reached out and patted my hand. "Relax. If there was anything going on they'd let us know. Bad shit doesn't always happen, Parker." She gave my hand a quick squeeze before letting it go.

I took a deep breath. She was right. I needed to stop living like disaster was going to be around every corner. It's hard, though, with all that I'd been through.

"You're right. It's hard sometimes to realize that my life might not actually end in pain. That I have this happiness and love that I found in Arya. And soon our child. It's crazy to me sometimes."

Pearl leaned back in her chair and nodded. "I understand. Granted, I didn't personally go through what you and Arya both did, but I experienced her pain. A mother feels her child's heartache deep in her soul. No matter how young or old they are. But you." She shook her head. "All that you've been through, you deserve happiness and love. I don't know someone more deserving."

I picked at the rim of my coffee cup. Deserving was something I had always struggled with. After being told I was worthless my entire life and struggling to survive, love seemed wasted on me. I believed what my parents said, or rather didn't say. I couldn't remember them ever saying they loved me. I learned to love how I was loved: not at all. Thankfully, I now had some amazing people in my life who were teaching me what it was like to not hate myself, to not want to curl up and die, or get so angry that I saw red. I was learning what it was like to love.

"I'm getting there. I'm not sure I'll ever deserve

Arya's patience and kindness, but her love—I'll take it." Pearl smiled at my words and started gathering up her trash.

"What do you say, Parker? Ready to go have a baby?"

I stood up fast, almost sending the chair tumbling behind me. Pearl and I both laughed.

"I take that as a yes."

I grinned and led the way. To my child. The love of my life. My future.

***

I was glad I'd taken the break, even though I thought about Arya the entire time. Pearl and I never really sat and talked just the two of us, and I was relieved to know that she thought I deserved Arya. No matter how many therapy sessions I had, doubt was a part of my personality. I doubted whether I could be a good father. I hadn't exactly had the best role model, but I decided I wouldn't be anything like him. If I didn't do anything he did, that had to be something, right?

We made our way down the long hallway to the sound of babies crying and monitors beeping. I smiled and my heart swelled thinking about holding my little girl in my arms. I could do this whole father thing.

Pearl patted my shoulder as if she knew what I was thinking.

"We're back, sweetie," Pearl said as we entered Arya's room.

It was empty. My heart, which had been just swelling with thoughts of happiness and joy, sank.

"Mr. Matthews. Mrs. Danvers." The nurse from earlier stood in the doorway.

"Where is she?" I tried to stay calm but my voice was shaky and a few octaves too high. The nurse backed up a bit but stood her ground.

"Parker, calm down." Pearl gripped my hand in hers. I felt her shaking too. We were holding each other together. Barely. Trying not to succumb to our worst fears.

"There was an emergency. They were both whisked off to surgery. The baby's heart rate got dangerously low. Arya was having trouble breathing. We didn't want to lose them. We had no choice." The nurse took a deep breath.

I closed my eyes and saw Arya's beautiful face. Her smile. I heard her laugh and tried not to crumble. I wasn't angry or scared. I felt defeated. Broken. My life was in that operating room and once again it was out of my control.

"Where are they? Can I go in to be with Arya?" I took another shaky breath and tried to think rationally.

"Well, the surgery has already started, but I can take you to the waiting room by the operating room.

That way as soon as they are out you will be there." She offered me a small smile of reassurance.

Pearl and I followed behind her, her squeaky shoes filling the silence. Pearl hadn't spoken a word but silent tears streamed down her face. Once we made it to the waiting area, Pearl sat down and wept, face in her hands.

I sat beside her and rubbed her back, letting my own tears fall.

"They're going to be okay," I said confidently.

"You think so?" Pearl looked at me, her eyes bloodshot and red.

"I know so. You know why?"

Pearl shook her head.

"Because Arya is strong. She's a fighter. She fought for her sobriety. For her life, back when she could have gone any other way. Arya won't let anything happen to our child and she'd be damned if she missed out on anything." I smiled and wiped a tear that had fallen off my cheek.

"You're a good man, Parker." She gripped my knee.

Just then, the doors to the waiting room swung open and the doctor came in carrying a pink-wrapped bundle. I shot off the chair, sending it back against the wall.

"Parker, I'd like you to meet your daughter."

She handed me the baby, and I looked down her pudgy face. She was beautiful like Arya, and then she opened her eyes and stared right at me and all I saw was Emily, my sister, staring back at me. I didn't try to hide it. I wept as I pressed kisses against her face. She was perfect and she was mine to love and cherish forever. To show the world and teach how to be the best human being possible.

"Arya?" I looked up at the doctor.

"She's going to be absolutely fine. She had to be put under, but she's strong. A real fighter. You should be able to see her shortly." Dr. Sanderson patted my shoulder. "Your daughter is beautiful. Congratulations. A nurse will be right out to take her." She walked away.

"Doc!" I yelled after her. Dr. Sanderson turned to face me.

"Thanks for taking care of my girls."

"My pleasure." She smiled and continued walking.

"Oh, my word, my granddaughter is gorgeous." Pearl pulled away the blanket and counted her toes. I laughed.

"You want to hold her?"

"Yes!" She held out her arms and I placed baby Emily in her arms.

Watching Pearl fuss and coo over her granddaughter, the pure joy that was on her face, I knew that this was my greatest creation. A mistake that turned into something beautiful. A child to love. A child to watch grow. A child to show how wonderful this world could be.

CHAPTER EIGHTEEN

Arya

As I opened my eyes, they fought to focus. My head spun as the room around me started to come into view. I heard the beeping of the machines and my hands instinctively went to my stomach.

Emily. Emergency C-section. My heart rate quickened as I gripped my stomach. It wasn't hard; there was no feeling of Emily moving. I was empty. She was gone.

Putting my hands beside me, I tried to sit up as panic set in. My stomach pulled and sharp, shooting pain radiated through me.

"Hey, settle down, sweetie. You just had surgery." I followed the voice to the nurse next to me who was checking my equipment. She gently placed me back down in the bed and tucked me back in.

My thoughts focused on Emily. Was she alive? God, please let her be okay. "The baby." My voice cracked.

"Is she…?"

"Perfect?" The door to the hospital room opened and Parker walked in, holding a pink bundle. "Yes, she's perfect, just like her mother." He placed a kiss to my lips as the nurse helped me sit up. Parker placed Emily in my arms and my eyes instantly welled up with tears. I looked at her sweet face. Felt her little hands in mine. She was soft. Gorgeous, and she was ours.

"Oh, my God," I whispered as I stroked my finger down her soft face. "I thought I was going to lose her." My tears fell. I remembered everything now. The medicine they gave me and the reaction I had. There was nothing like hearing the nurses and doctors panicking around you and not being able to control anything. I'd feared I'd never see Emily's face. Or never see Parker again. I whimpered at the memory.

"Hey." Parker sat down in the chair next to me and rubbed my leg. "You're both here. Healthy and beautiful. Don't think about what could have happened."

I smiled at the man who once lived in constant pain. Who struggled to see the beauty in life due to all the loss he had experienced. He was different now. Stronger, wiser. Parker Matthews was healing, and it was a beautiful thing to see.

"I can only imagine how you felt coming back to see me and hearing what happened. I'm so sorry to put you through that." Emily stirred in my arms and I started rocking her.

Parker sat back further in the chair and smiled. I wasn't sure what had come over him. I was just talking about the possibly that Emily and I wouldn't be here any longer, and he was smiling? Healing was great, but anyone who had gone through what he had and then was told his girlfriend and unborn child were whisked off into surgery would have a reaction other than smiling.

"Why are you smiling, you're scaring me!" I half laughed and fought back the tears that kept trying to make their appearance.

"I'm not going to lie and say that I didn't fear the worst. Even sitting down in the cafeteria with your mother, I couldn't help but think about you and how you were doing every second. When I came into your room and heard what happened, my heart dropped but it wasn't the same. I had your mother thinking she was going to lose her only daughter, her unborn grandchild, and the only thing I could think about was making sure that she had hope because that was something I never had. It was always doom and gloom. Chaos and tragedy one after the other." He sighed.

"It wasn't the same as what?" I questioned.

"As before. When everything threatened to strangle me, and take away my happiness. Because all those other things in my life, the moments that I held on to that I felt defined who I was, were nothing."

"Don't say that. They were all something," I argued. I didn't like the idea of Parker thinking that his past meant nothing. Even what I'd been through, being raped and becoming an alcoholic, was all a part of me. It had molded me into who I was today.

"Sure. They meant something. They were a stepping stone to us. To our story and happily ever after. Every story has a beginning, middle, and an end." Parker stood and took Emily from my arms. He removed the pink blanket that covered her and placed her back in my arms. "Will you be my end, Arya?"

I looked down at Emily, whose onesie said Will you Marry My Daddy?

Parker got down on one knee and opened a ring box.

I was speechless.

"I don't have much else to say, but will you marry me, Arya? Will you be my happiness for the rest of my life?"

With tears in my eyes, I tried to keep it together but it was a fruitless effort. I had no words. My mind shot to our future in our new house with Emily growing up and more children running around. It was how I'd pictured my life ever since I met Parker. It was all I'd dreamed.

"If you need to think about it, it's fine. I just thought…." As if knowing what was going on, Emily started crying. I held her over my shoulder and patted her butt, cooing into her ear.

"Hey, sweet girl. It's okay. Mommy's going to marry your daddy and we're going to live happily ever after."

Parker jumped up and put the ring on my finger.

"You sure you won't regret this?" I joked as I looked at the beautiful solitaire diamond. It was simple, but stunning. The diamond glistening on my finger that I couldn't help moving around. Parker laughed, smiled, and pressed a kiss to my forehead.

"There is nothing about you that I will ever regret. You have been my greatest journey. My greatest heartache. My greatest triumph, Arya Danvers. Don't you ever forget that. You saved me from myself. You gave me the strength to want to be a better man."

I wanted more than words from Parker, and he gave me that with his actions. He got treatment for his PTSD, bought a house for us, and asked me to marry him. His words held magic, meaning, and hope. Everything he said seeped love even when his poetry held the pain he experienced. Underneath it all, deep within the crevices of Parker Matthews, was just a man who wanted to be loved, a man who wanted someone to love.

I'd love him till the end of time. And I knew he'd love Emily and me too.

CHAPTER NINETEEN

Parker

I'd never been so nervous in my life. I'd been in war countless times, but bringing home a newborn baby left me sweating like a damn pig.

"Relax, it's going to be okay." Arya smiled at me as she and Emily were being wheeled from the hospital.

"What if we screw this up?" I stopped at the car door, then turned to look at her, the panic fully setting in. "What if she hates us?"

Arya let out a small laugh as I helped her out of the wheelchair. Emily was sound asleep in her arms, peaceful and content. She didn't look like she could hate anyone. Let alone do any wrong. She had me hooked already, wrapped around her little finger, and she was barely a week old.

"She won't hate us. Take a breath." Arya's eyes found mine and I did as she said. "That better?"

I nodded. "Let's get her in the car." I took Emily

from her arms and placed the infant in the car seat. Like a pro, I buckled her in.

"Where'd you learn how to do that?" Arya asked as she made sure she was buckled in securely.

"May have taken lessons from your brother." I winked as I helped her in the car.

"You're amazing, you know that?" Arya gripped my hand that was clicking her seat belt.

"Haven't always been."

"And that's okay. It makes these moments we have together that much sweeter." She leaned in and kissed my cheek. "Let's take our baby home."

Home. I'd never had a place I really thought of as home. Rainey and I tried to build one together, but everything felt so disconnected. I never was able to settle and enjoy much of life without thinking of the what-ifs and dwelling on the past. I'd realized though that home isn't a place. It's a feeling. A person. A state of mind.

Arya and Emily were my home. They were what I had been waiting for.

"Yes, let's go home." Slipping Arya's hand in mine, I drove incredibly slowly to the place where we would raise our children and put down roots. For the first time in forever, I had a place to call home.

***

Emily didn't believe in sleeping. Which made for two very tired parents.

I was functioning on a mere three hours of sleep and it was sporadic at best. I had to be at work in about a half hour but nothing could take the place of what being a father felt like. Every time she looked at me, I wanted to give her everything. I'd take the moon from the sky for this little girl.

It made me question how my parents could have been so incredibly dysfunctional and uncaring toward my sister and me. But as I held Emily in my arms and watched her sleep, I realized it wasn't me or Emily or anything we did wrong. It was them. Their issues that caused them to check out from various aspects of life that mattered, including their own children. It was easier to not care than to realize what a shitty environment we were all in. Something in me lifted, like a weight I'd been carrying around my entire life. I was good enough. I hadn't been a perfect child or person, no one was, but I was worthy of my parents' love and deep down somewhere they loved us. And I forgave them for everything.

I was free; forgiveness gave me that. I forgave not only my parents but also myself for all the shit I put everyone in my life through. I had to. For Emily and Arya, to be the best version of myself I could be. And for me, so I could live and finally be happy.

"Let me take her, you're going to be late for work."

Arya stood in the doorway to Emily's nursery, her hair going every which way, still in the same pajamas from the morning even though it was five o'clock in the afternoon. She'd never looked more beautiful.

"Why are you looking at me like that?" She giggled.

"You're beautiful, that's all." I patted Emily's butt as we rocked in the rocking chair.

"All right, you already won me over and I said I'd marry you. No need to go all crazy now." Arya took Emily from my arms and held her out in front of her.

"Hi, sweet pea. Daddy is being silly." Of course, Emily said nothing but stared at her.

"Even she knows it's true." I kissed Arya's forehead. "I'll be home in the morning. I hope you get some rest tonight."

"Be safe," she said.

"Always am. I love you."

"I love you too." As I walked out of the nursery I couldn't help but steal a glance back at the woman of my dreams and little girl who stole my heart and wasn't even two months old yet.

Nothing was perfect, but my life was damn near close.

***

"Man, you look like you need a week of sleep," Ross

said as he sipped his coffee. I held the large cup in my hand, the burning sensation keeping me awake. It was my fourth cup of the night and if I'd been anyone else, I might have been jumping off the walls, but coffee barely did anything to me anymore. Coffee was in my veins.

"I do."

Ross shook his head before replying. "This is why I'm not having any more kids. I value my sleep."

I laughed. "Yeah. I value a lot of things, but being a parent, it's unlike anything else, man. You have this little person that kind of looks like you that steals your sleep, pees and poops all the time."

"Sounds wonderful." Ross rolled his eyes. "I remember those days. I didn't love them. I was young when my daughter was born. Did some stupid shit, but I don't want to almost mess up another kid again."

"I'm sure you didn't mess her up."

"I haven't seen her. I wouldn't know." Ross shrugged. My heart ached for him. I couldn't imagine having a child and not seeing her.

"I hope you get to. Being a father is the greatest feeling in the world." I stared out the window and thought of Emily and Arya. My phone buzzed and an incoming picture of Emily in the bath filled my screen.

Ross looked over and let out a small laugh. "She is a cutie, though. Thank God she looks like Arya." We both laughed.

"Hey, so you know that Arya and I are getting

married...." Ross nodded and took another sip of his coffee. "I was wondering if you'd be a groomsman?" I ran my fingers through my hair that I still kept a bit longer.

"Seriously?" Ross looked at me wide-eyed.

"I know we don't know each other well, if it's weird it's fine. I just know you'd have my back and all that...." I sounded like I was asking him to go steady. Was I sweating? I thought I was.

"Man." Ross awkwardly tried to give me a hug over the center console. "Of course. I'll always have your back. We're more than partners, we're friends."

I wasn't going to cry. Not here in front of Ross, but goddammit did I feel my eyes getting misty.

"I'm going to throw you the best bachelor party ever!" He pulled out his phone and started texting. Gone were the tears, replaced with sheer panic.

"Nothing crazy. My brother-in-law is my best man." I laughed and took a breath, a sigh of relief. I didn't have many friends; after losing Jon and Cooper I'd shut myself off from everyone, but slowly I was starting to build friendships. No one would ever be able to take Jon and Cooper's place and I wasn't trying to do that. I was trying to rebuild myself, my life that had fallen to shambles. The foundation was stronger, built on loss and pain, but that's where the strength came from, the perseverance, and I knew this time it wouldn't falter.

CHAPTER TWENTY

Arya

It'd been a year and a half since Parker proposed. He would have married me in my pajamas with baby spit on my shirt if I let him. Trust me, I thought about it many times, just eloping with him, Emily, and me to some island and enjoying the sun with my little family, but I couldn't do that to my parents or to myself.

My parents had been through so much with me and never given up. This day seemed like a milestone, a success that may have not come if I'd succumbed to my addiction. I wasn't saying I was weak. That's a stigma surrounding any mental illness that bothers me—*weakness*. It wasn't weakness. I considered it strength. That you were so strong that pain could be a challenge to process, like my rape. Like Parker's childhood and time at war and losing his friends. We both held so much strength it just took us longer to find it and to find each other.

Parker was worth the wait, and all the things that came before him were necessary to reach this point. He was my hope, my constant even when he wasn't. He held the key to my heart and gave me one of the greatest gifts: Emily.

"Momma, up!" Emily held her hands up to me. I was already in my wedding dress, a tight lace gown that showed off all my hard work post-baby. Okay, so all of me waiting eighteen months to get married wasn't just for my parents, it was for me too. I wanted the dress, the venue, the dancing and good food. I wanted my family and friends to celebrate with me. I had found love, happiness, and I wanted everyone to know.

"No, Em. Mommy's all dressed up." My mother swooped in and picked up Emily, who still was reaching out for me. You'd think she was a momma's girl, but she wasn't. She loved Parker more than anything in the world. I loved watching her eyes light up as she stood at the window watching his truck pull in from work. She'd screech and dance at the door until he came in and swung her around.

They were perfect and all mine. Well, Parker was about to be, forever.

I kissed Emily's cheek. My mother started sniffing.

"Don't start, Mom, you know I don't want to mess up my makeup." I started fanning at my face, trying to dry the tears that were welling.

"I know, baby. I just can't believe this day is finally here. You look stunning."

Emily wiggled out of her arms and ran to Mona, who was finishing getting ready.

"Thank you. I can't believe this day is finally here either." I took a deep breath.

"I'm proud of you." She put her hands on my shoulders and looked me right in the eyes. "Everything you both have been through never stopped you from going after what you both truly deserved, and that's each other. Love. Happiness. I'm so blessed to have you as my daughter."

The tears fell and there was no fanning them away.

"Thank you for being supportive and never giving up on me."

"Never." She gripped my hands and squeezed. "Your path was exactly what it needed to be for you. It got you here and you overcame the challenges. That's what matters most. So, don't dwell on the past or think about the what-ifs, because baby girl, you made it. You have your happily ever after." She kissed my cheek. "Now let's go get that hunk of man who is probably about to pass out."

"Yup. According to Justin he is about to put a hole in the floor, he's been pacing so much."

We laughed.

"Well, let's do this." I looked at myself in the mirror one last time.

"You look amazing. Parker is going to lose it when he sees you," Mona said.

"It's time." My dad held out his arm and I linked

mine through it. He patted my hand, and we walked toward the entryway to the church. The music played and everything settled in my mind. There were no nerves. No regrets, or wondering if I was making the right choice, because I knew I was. I had never been more certain of anything in my life.

I heard laughter as Emily ran down the aisle ever so gracefully, and right into her father's arms. He kissed her cheek and placed her on my mother's lap.

The music changed to "The Man I Love" by Billie Holiday, and I knew it was time. It wasn't a traditional song but it was how I felt about Parker. He made me smile. He was strong and fierce. And I'd never roam or leave his side. He was my forever and I was his.

My father gave me a smile and we began walking forward.

Everyone stood and snapped pictures, but I didn't care, my eyes were on the man I was going to marry.

Parker stood at the end of the aisle, and as soon as he saw me he started crying. Then I started crying. This wasn't a few tears, it was heartfelt and real. The emotion that poured from him was overwhelming. But damn did it feel good to be loved.

When we made it to the end, my father kissed my cheek before Parker took my hands in his.

The rest went by in a whirlwind. Words of undying love and promises were made that I knew we'd keep.

"Parker has prepared a little poem for his new wife." My attention shot to Parker, who closed his eyes and took a deep breath. I knew he still wrote. There were notebooks scattered around our house that he would often pick up to jot down words or thoughts. I never asked to read anything. If he wanted to share, I knew he would.

"Arya and I fell in love with each other over words. Today I'd like to share with everyone how much she means to me. I've never been good at expressing myself except through writing. That's helped me to open up and find happiness in this wonderfully caring, compassionate, and beautiful woman." Parker took my hands and cleared his throat.

"There is no such thing as perfection.

Flaws, scars, and mistakes fill my past.

But then, I looked into your eyes and saw what I had been searching for all along.

Peace. Happiness. Joy.

Love never made sense until you came into my life.

Life never seemed worth living until you opened my eyes to its beauty.

Beauty seemed superficial until I saw your smile for the first time.

You saved me. When all I wanted to do was crumble.

You put me back together when I shattered into a thousand pieces.

My love for you is stronger than anything I knew possible.

My love for you is the strength I needed to survive."

I gripped Parker's cheeks in my hands.

"I love you, Parker Matthews. And I'd save you a thousand times over."

"Let me do some saving now, sweetheart," Parker interrupted.

And with that, Parker and I became husband and wife. Till death did us part. Because that's what it would take to tear us apart. Our love was forged in our struggle, but I found that when you struggled and fought for what you wanted, it made it even sweeter when you realized that you'd made it.

Parker and I made it. And our love was proof of that.

EPILOGUE

One Year Later
Parker

I pushed Emily in the stroller. She had promptly passed out after seeing Santa Claus. While I'd once hated the holidays, I now cherished them deeply. Seeing Christmas through the eyes of a child brought a sense of joy and excitement that I'd never known existed.

"I think she'll sleep well tonight." Arya rubbed her swollen stomach that held our son. He wasn't planned, but what in life was? We wanted a house full of kids and that's what we were getting.

My PTSD, while it would never fully go away, was being managed. I saw a therapist, wrote, worked out, and had support. Well, I had support and actually let them support me. I hadn't had a drink in years, and that helped keep my mind clear. I loved my job, and Ross and I remained partners and kicked ass together. We made a great team.

"I think so too. Question is, will you get any sleep tonight?" I rubbed her back and she groaned.

"If Alex here stops kicking, maybe."

"Stubborn like his father. You're welcome." I winked.

"I'm going to run to the bathroom, again, for the third time in an hour." Arya stood on her tiptoes and kissed my lips. "Be back as fast as my swollen feet will let me."

I sat down at the nearest table in the food court and watched her walk away. I'd never tire of looking at her, or kissing her, or loving her.

"Parker?" I looked up and there stood Rainey, her own stomach round and her cheeks rosy. But what I noticed most was the smile on her face. Last time I'd seen her, we buried Emily and there weren't smiles. Just grief. Pain. Regrets. There was none of that. The past was just that—a distant memory. A time when we were young and had fallen in love with hopes and dreams. We were people who had changed and grown in different directions.

Now we were different.

"Rainey." I stood up and gave her a quick hug. "You look amazing. How is everything?"

"Things are great." She rubbed her stomach and smiled. "Baby number two is on the way."

"Me too." I lowered the canopy on the stroller and Rainey looked down at Emily.

"She's gorgeous, Parker. She looks a lot like you."

"Thanks. She's got some of my attitude. Not sure what I'm going to do when she's a teenager." We laughed. A calmness came over me. It wasn't awkward or tense, there was peace.

"Well, I came down here for a snack while Levi haggles with the cell phone salesman." She shook her head, a slight grin stretching across her face. "It was great to see you."

"You too."

I watched her walk away, my past that had haunted me for so long. I didn't feel regret, sadness, or any pain. Just contentment that Rainey was happy, because despite all that I had put her through, she finally got what she deserved: happiness.

"Rainey?" I called after her.

She turned around.

"I'm sorry. For everything. Will you ever be able to forgive me?"

"Parker, I forgave you forever ago. Be happy. Love your girls."

"Thank you." I waved one last time as the woman I had once been in love with walked away.

At the end of the day, we all deserved to be happy. I made the mistake of putting my happiness in other people's hands when it came from no one else but myself.

I chose my happiness, and while it wasn't my high school sweetheart, it was the woman who was made for me. Arya Danvers was my everything.

ACKNOWLEDGMENTS

Gosh, I don't even know where to start. This series wrecked me in the most glorious way. I wrote it all while my husband was deployed (our third deployment). This deployment was easier than the others because after a while, the military life becomes like second nature. He's been in for thirteen years. The entire time we've been together. You learn how to fix things that break around the house. When your basement floods for the third time you literally hike up your pants and trudge through (true story). However, the emotions were real. The tears, the thoughts, all came from somewhere deep within me. Just because this deployment was my third, doesn't mean I don't have my moments because I can tell you that after the third flood in my basement I may have sat in the middle of the water and cried. Not one of my finer moments but it's the truth. The ugly truth about how military life can impact people.

I want to acknowledge and thank every single

military personnel and their family for their sacrifice. Missed anniversaries and holidays are always a major hurdle but I think what I realized as this series came to an end and as my husband is due home any day now, it's the little things that are missed. The binge-watching Netflix or trips to the grocery store. It's the crawling into bed with the one you love and despite their snores and hogging the covers, you feel comfortable and safe. So, for giving up those little things, for waiting a year or more to feel comfortable and secure again in your own home, I thank you. It isn't easy to say goodbye to someone you love and sometimes it can be even harder when they come back. You can lose yourself in waiting for them. Their phone call or e-mail. That's where Rainey came from. The person who puts their all in their loved one but struggles with herself. That's reality sometimes and it can be a challenge to overcome that hurdle.

Military life isn't for everyone, but we are strong, an unconventional family that is bounded through loss, blood, and tears. A solid foundation that even when we feel like falling, we get right back up and kick ass. Together. Strength is our foundation and love for our country and those who serve runs through our veins.

Thank you for reading my story, for loving Rainey, Levi, Parker, and Arya, because at the end of the day, military life is messy and chaotic, hell even heartbreaking, but I know I wouldn't trade a single tear or goodbye for anything in the world.

ABOUT THE AUTHOR

Gen Ryan is an international best-selling author that spends her days as a forensic psychologist filling the minds of college students with everything they need to know to be good at their jobs. From profiling to interrogation and ending with her absolute favorite, serial killers. Her nights, however, are spent crafting stories that will tear a reader's heart out and twist their minds at the same time.

She brings a unique twist to romance, a twist always rooted somewhere deep inside the character's psyche.

Follow Gen:

FACEBOOK: WWW.FACEBOOK.COM/GENRYANAUTHOR
WEBSITE: WWW.GENRYANBOOKS.COM/
TWITTER: TWITTER.COM/GENRYAN15

ABOUT THE PUBLISHER

Hot Tree Publishing opened its doors in 2015 with an aspiration to bring quality fiction to the world of readers. With the initial focus on romance and a wide spread of romance subgenres, we envision opening up to alternative genres in the near future.

Firmly seated in the industry as a leading editing provider to independent authors and small publishing houses, Hot Tree Publishing is the sister company to Hot Tree Editing, founded in 2012. Having established in-house editing and promotions, plus having a well-respected market presence, Hot Tree Publishing endeavors to be a leader in bringing quality stories to the world of readers.

Interested in discovering more amazing reads brought to you by Hot Tree Publishing? Head over to the website for information:

WWW.HOTTREEPUBLISHING.COM

Milton Keynes UK
Ingram Content Group UK Ltd.
UKHW040658050124
435493UK00001B/42